"Do you want to leave?" Rhys asked

How simple it would be to tell him yes, she had had enough.... But she couldn't do it. "The advertisement was misleading," she stammered, playing for time.

Rhys broke in roughly. "You least of all the applicants should complain of conditions here. You insisted on accepting the position."

"It must have been galling for you to have to accept me."

His lips twisted. "Are you looking for compliments, Miss Wood?"

"No." She held her head up. "And I'll stay."

For a moment a strange expression crossed his face, and her knees trembled violently. She was mad, she thought wildly. There was going to be nothing but trouble for her here and she was a fool for not recognizing it.

Other titles by

ANNE MATHER
IN HARLEQUIN PRESENTS

FORBIDDEN 221
COME RUNNING 224
DEVIL IN VELVET 234
LOREN'S BABY 250
ROOTED IN DISHONOUR 254
PROUD HARVEST 262
SCORPIONS' DANCE 266
FOLLOW THY DESIRE 269
CAPTIVE DESTINY 278
CHARADE IN WINTER 281
FALLEN ANGEL 287
MELTING FIRE 306
THE JUDAS TRAP 322
LURE OF EAGLES 329
APOLLO'S SEED 335
HELL OR HIGH WATER 347

Other titles by

ANNE MATHER
IN HARLEQUIN ROMANCES

CHARLOTTE'S HURRICANE 1487
LORD OF ZARACUS 1574
THE RELUCTANT GOVERNESS 1600
MASQUERADE 1631
AUTUMN OF THE WITCH 1656

Many of these titles, and other titles in the Harlequin
Romance series, are available at your local
bookseller. For a free catalogue listing all available
Harlequin Presents and Harlequin Romances, send
your name and address to:

HARLEQUIN READER SERVICE,
M.P.O. Box 707,
Niagara Falls, N.Y. 14302
Canadian address:
Stratford, Ontario, Canada N5A 6W2

ANNE MATHER

devil's mount

Harlequin Books

TORONTO • LONDON • LOS ANGELES • AMSTERDAM
SYDNEY • HAMBURG • PARIS • STOCKHOLM • ATHENS • TOKYO

Harlequin Presents edition published September 1977
ISBN 0-373-10205-4

Second printing March 1980
Original hardcover edition published in 1976
by Mills & Boon Limited

CHAPTER ONE

The Viking raised the silver goblet to his lips and drank deeply of the fiery spirit, his flashing blue eyes raking the faces around him, searching for that one face which could bring the light of proud possession to their depths. He tossed back his long hair, his white teeth strong and eager as he bit into the flesh of . . .

"Mr. Hollister's waiting for you, you know, Julie!"

Nancy Walker's voice was stridently intrusive, and Julie turned from the window impatiently as the lusty Viking became once more the telephone engineer who was presently taking his tea break across the road from the offices of Hollister, Barnes and Hollister, Solicitors, Commissioners for Oaths, etc.

"He won't appreciate you wasting your time day-dreaming over long-haired layabouts when he's waiting to give you dictation," went on Nancy, walking to the window, her mouth pulling down at the corners as the young engineer raised his thumbs towards her. "Honestly, Julie, do you want to lose this job?"

Julie sighed and reached for her shorthand notebook. How could she explain that she had been paying scant attention to what was actually going on in the street outside? Her thoughts had been far from the doings of a post office engineer repairing the cable down a hole in the pavement. She had been indulging in her favourite fantasy, transported back to Saxon times, a maiden ravished by her Viking lord, who in turn fell in love with her . . .

"I don't think I'm cut out to work in a solicitor's office," she volunteered, getting to her feet. "I mean, there's more to life than death and divorce, isn't there?"

Nancy made a frustrated sound. "Like that young man outside, I suppose."

"No, not necessarily." Julie shook her head, her long corn-coloured hair swinging loosely about her shoulders. "The work just doesn't interest me, that's all." She hesitated. "Nancy, don't you ever get bored?"

Nancy looked scandalised. Although she was married, she had worked for Hollister, Barnes and Hollister for the past fifteen years, and Julie guessed her words were tantamount to anarchy in Nancy's ears.

"You don't appreciate how lucky you are to have a job at all," she exclaimed, pacing to stand before Julie's desk. "Are you aware that a great number of young people can't find employment of any kind?"

Julie nodded. "I know, I know."

"Besides, I thought you liked typing. When you concentrate on what you're doing, you're pretty good."

This was praise indeed, and Julie smiled. "I do like typing," she said. "It's what I'm typing I find so dull! So— I think about other things."

"What other things?"

The office door opened and Jennifer Lewis, Mr. Barnes' secretary, put her head round. "Do you know where—"she began, seeing only Nancy at first, but then her eyes travelled on to Julie, and she grimaced at the younger girl. "Mr. Hollister's screaming his head off. What've you been doing, Julie? He's madder than a bull in—"

"That will do, Jennifer." Nancy straightened away from the desk. "You'd better hurry along, Julie. Or you may find you have no choice in the matter of occupations."

Julie hurried, and suffered Hector Hollister's vituperative response to her apologies before he got down to the business of dictation. But the letters he dictated she had heard a dozen times before – *the deeds of your late mother's property are now in*

6

our possession, and if you could arrange to call at this office – my client absolutely refuses to consider even temporary custody of the child to your client – the insurance due on the said property, etc. etc. . . . She could feel her thoughts drifting, and she had to concentrate heavily to get down everything he said without adding comments of her own.

Travelling home on the underground that evening, strap-hanging as usual, she tried to review the dissatisfaction which seemed to be getting stronger day by day. At what point had her work at Hollisters become so untenable? She had been there seven months, the seven months since she had left secretarial college, and to begin with it had not seemed so bad. But perhaps familiarity had bred contempt, as they say, and it was a fact that she was contemptuous of Hector Hollister. A man so polite with his clients could be amazingly rude to his staff, and Julie was tired of fending off his familiarity.

But perhaps more than anything, her discontent had manifested itself at Laura's wedding three weeks ago. Not that she envied her sister. Getting married at nineteen was not her idea of making a life for herself, and although Laura seemed ridiculously happy with her area sales representative, Julie thought she was crazy. They wouldn't have a penny to spare once they had covered the mortgage repayments on their three-bedroomed semi in Barnet, and Laura would have to work forever to maintain a decent standard of living.

Of course, Julie knew that her mother hoped she would soon decide to get married. Since becoming a widow five years ago, Mrs. Wood had not found it easy to support herself and her two daughters. But she had ensured that they both gained secretarial ability, and now that Laura was married, she was looking forward to the day when she could sell their small house in Romford and go to live with her widowed sister in Southend. Only Julie stood in the way — and as Julie was over eighteen, she should be considering her future, or so Mrs.

7

Wood believed.

But her mother's ideas of considering Julie's future usually included consideration of Mark Roberts. Mark lived in the same road as the Woods, he came from a well-respected family, and he had just completed his teacher training. More to the point, he had always shown an interest in Julie, and now that he had got a teaching post at a nearby comprehensive school, his attentions were getting more serious.

Julie sighed. She liked Mark. She always had. But he was only a little over medium height, and stocky, with gingery hair and a tendency to make pompous statements about life in general, and teenagers in particular. Consequently, Julie found it difficult to take him seriously, and certainly she didn't love him. She had come to the conclusion that she would never find anybody to live up to her expectations, and was quite prepared to remain single for the rest of her life. But not as secretary to Hector Hollister!

She allowed her thoughts to drift, and soon the swaying tube became the deck of a Viking vessel, the buzz of voices oarsmen stroking their craft through white-flecked waves. She was clinging to the dragon's head carved on the prow of the ship, which served to terrorise those they came to plunder, and the scornful voice in her ear was that of the helmsman, exhorting her to get behind him . . .

"Will you let me pass?"

The angry voice penetrated the fantasy and she gulped and coloured in embarrassment as a bowler-hatted businessman strove to squeeze past her to reach the doors. She shrank back into a corner, controlling her own annoyance when the point of his umbrella dug into her leg, and then stooped to pick up the newspaper he had dropped. The doors were closing behind him by this time, and she was left with the paper in her hand, feeling rather foolish.

There was now a vacant seat further along the compartment, and she went to take it, deliberately opening the newspaper to give herself some privacy. It was *The Times*, not the sort of paper she usually read, her mother's tastes running to the *Daily Mirror* or the *Express*. But anything was better than sitting staring at her fellow travellers for another handful of stations, and she found her eyes indifferently scanning the Situations Vacant column.

Someone wanted a nurse/companion for a trip to Australia. That sounded interesting. All expenses paid aboard a luxury liner. But she had no nursing experience, so that didn't help her. Someone else wanted a governess. An Asian family, it said, living in Central Africa, wanted an English girl to tutor their two children. Julie sighed. Obviously, she had chosen the wrong occupation. And yet she couldn't honestly see herself in the role of governess.

Wealthy recluse requires competent secretary.

The words fairly jumped out of the page at her, and she read them again. "Wealthy recluse requires a competent secretary. Applicant must be an accurate typist, and have a shorthand speed of up to 100 words a minute."

Julie's brows drew together. That was all it said, apart from giving a telephone number to call for enquiries. How tantalising! Who on earth could it be? And where might the post be? What a fantastic opportunity for somebody.

The train was pulling out of Elm Park when she looked up. Hers was the next station. She had no time to re-read the advertisement right now, or even to consider why she might want to read it once more. Flinging her long tartan scarf over her shoulder, she left the train at Hornchurch, the edition of *The Times* still clutched in her hand.

Outside the station, the October evening was faintly misty, the street lamps casting pools of milky light, frost already glistening on the pavements. Julie still had a bus ride to make before she was home, and throughout the journey she thought about the advertisement. A wealthy recluse! She could guess what that would mean. Some rich old man living in the lap of luxury on some remote Caribbean island. How marvellous! Lots of sun and sea and good food. That was really living! Not just scraping along in some suburban semi, with every mailman's step heralding the arrival of another bill you can't pay.

She wrinkled her nose dejectedly. Of course, there would be dozens of applicants. Every half-baked secretary in London would jump at a position like that. But it wasn't the half-baked ones she had to worry about. It was the sleek sophisticated business girls in their late twenties or early thirties, who all looked as if they'd just stepped from the pages of *Vogue* magazine, and had typing and shorthand speeds to match.

Julie surveyed her reflection critically in the darkened glass of the window beside her. She wasn't bad looking really, but she wasn't at all sophisticated, and even her mother had had to admit that she didn't look eighteen. She sighed frustratedly. Her hair was all right. She could always put it up or have it cut or something. But those wide brown eyes were definitely too ingenuous, and her mouth was too vulnerable. She hunched her shoulders as she glimpsed the reflections of two schoolboys across the aisle, watching her with evident amusement. Why was she bothering anyway? She hadn't even thought about making the telephone call yet.

Her evening meal was already on the table when she let herself into the house in Eastman Road. Her mother came through from the kitchen as she was shedding her coat and scarf in the hall indicating that Julie should start without her.

"It's the Autumn Fair at the junior school this evening, Julie," she explained, pausing at the foot of the stairs, "and I've promised Mrs. Lomax that I'd go along and help out. So many of the parents don't seem to care about giving a helping hand. They send their children to school and think that's the end of it."

Julie draped the strap of her handbag over a hook on the hallstand. "Did you have a good day?"

Mrs. Wood worked at a local wool shop on a part-time basis, and supplemented the small pension her husband had left her in this way.

Now she nodded. "Fortunately, we haven't been run off our feet," she answered, "or I shouldn't be helping out tonight."

"Perhaps that's why more of the parents don't get involved," suggested Julie, walking towards the kitchen and the appetizing smell of steak and kidney pie. "Most wives have to work these days, and I expect they're glad to get their feet up when they get home."

Her mother made a disbelieving sound. "They're not too tired to go out playing bingo or keeping fit! Do you know Mrs. Laurence has actually joined a Yoga group!"

Julie hid a smile. Mrs. Laurence was at least fourteen stone, and to imagine her attempting the lotus position didn't bear thinking about.

Mrs. Wood went to get ready to go out and Julie seated herself at the kitchen table and tackled the steak and kidney pie with relish. There was a raspberry crumble to follow, and a cup of her mother's strong black coffee, and she rose from the table ruefully rubbing her flat stomach. Her mother's menus were definitely not calorie-conscious, and tomorrow lunchtime she would have to make do with two crispbreads and a lettuce leaf. Although it suited her mother to be plump, Julie had no intention of adding that drawback to what she considered to be her other disadvantages.

She washed her dishes, cleared the table, and then went through to the sitting room. A warm fire was burning in the grate, and she settled herself on the couch, flicking through the pages of a magazine. Mrs. Wood bustled in, tall and attractive in her grey tweed coat. Both her daughters resembled her more than their father, but with Julie it was only a physical resemblance.

"Well, I'm going," she said. "By the way," she dropped the copy of *The Times* beside Julie on the couch, "I found this hanging out of your coat pocket. I didn't know you bought *The Times*."

"I don't," said Julie, half guiltily, barely casting an eye in its direction. "I—er—someone dropped it on the train."

"And you picked it up!" Her mother looked scandalised. "Julie!"

Julie shook her head. "Are you going now, Mummy?"

Mrs. Wood looked as though she would have liked to say more, but bit her tongue. "Oh—yes. Yes, I'm going. I'll be home soon after nine, I expect. Is Mark coming round?"

"I hope not," replied Julie shortly, and her mother sighed.

"I heard from Mrs. Morton that Lucy saw Mark talking to Susan Thornton in the High Street on Saturday," she told her daughter reluctantly. "And you know what she's like. She's always had her eye on him."

"Good for her," observed Julie idly, turning another page of the magazine.

"Is that all you can say? Don't you care?"

"Not particularly." Julie looked up. "Aren't you going to be late?"

Mrs. Wood hesitated only a moment longer, and then with a stifled exclamation she marched to the door. "Goodbye, Julie," she said in a tight little voice, and Julie watched her go with resignation. She knew exactly what that tone of voice meant, and the prospect of several days of her mother's restrained politeness could stretch the nerves. But what could she do? She had no intention of marrying anyone just to satisfy her mother. And if her presence in the house was an inconvenience, then perhaps she ought to consider looking for a bed-sitter in town.

Her eyes alighted on the newspaper, and on impulse she picked it up and read the advertisement again. The telephone number indicated a central London address, and it gave no hours between which to call. She studied it for a few minutes longer, and then slid off the couch and walked out into the hall. Another second's hesitation, and she had lifted the receiver of the telephone and was dialling the number, not really knowing what she was going to say if anyone answered.

"Limerick Hotel!"

A receptionist's voice startled her out of her speculations. "Limerick Hotel?" she echoed faintly.

"That's right. Can I help you?"

"I—well, I'm ringing in answer to—"

"—the advertisement in *The Times*?" The receptionist did not sound surprised.

"Well—yes."

"Just a moment."

The line went dead, and for a moment Julie felt like hanging up before she committed herself further, but then the receptionist came on again: "You're through now."

"Hello. Who am I speaking to, please?"

It was a masculine voice, a young masculine voice, educated, yet with a faint accent which Julie couldn't quite place. She licked her lips.

"Oh—my name is Julie Wood," she introduced herself jerkily. "I'm enquiring about the position—as secretary."

"I see. And what are your qualifications, Miss Wood?"

"I have a typing speed of approximately seventy words a minute and my shorthand is upwards of a hundred."

"Impressive." He sounded faintly amused. "And why do you want this job, Miss Wood?"

"I—I'd like a change, that's all. I work in a solicitor's office at the moment, and the work is rather—"

"Dull?"

"Well, yes."

"And you don't think this position would be?"

Julie sighed. She didn't altogether like stating her reasons for applying for the job over the phone. She didn't know who was interviewing her, and he could have no idea who she was or whether indeed she was serious.

"I—just think it sounds rather interesting," she said lamely, and there was silence for a minute.

Then: "You will appreciate, Miss Wood, that we have had a great number of applications for this post already ..."

Here it came. The crunch. Julie stifled her disappointment.

"... and naturally, we are having to shortlist those who we believe may have something to offer."

"Of course," she managed in a small voice.

"That is why I am asking you these questions. An interview will follow if you are considered suitable."

Julie's spirits lifted again. "I see."

"To go on—what kind of salary did you have in mind for the job?"

Julie gasped. "I have no idea."

"You must have some idea. What is your present salary?"

Julie pursed her lips. "I don't think that's any concern of yours."

"Very well. I'll take it that it's less than two thousand a year." Julie gulped, and he went on: "Now—the post itself. I expect you're curious to know where it is."

"A little."

"That's perfectly natural. Well, I can't tell you the exact location at the moment for obvious reasons, but sufficient to say that you'll require the minimum amount of summer clothing. Does that appeal to you, Miss Wood?"

Julie's fingers were trembling as she clutched the receiver. A salary of two thousand pounds a year, and a place in the sun! Of course it appealed to her!

"It—it sounds very nice," she said, inadequately, and he laughed. She paused to wonder who he might be. A personal assistant perhaps? Or a public relations man? Clearly, he was too youthful to be her employer. Besides, wealthy recluses did not conduct conversations of this kind. They employed others to do it for them.

"How old are you, Miss Wood?"

His question startled her, and she chewed on her lower lip, wondering whether she ought to lie about her age. But if she did and she got an interview, that would kill her chances once and for all.

"Is—is that relevant?" she temporised.

"I think it might be."

"Oh! Well, I'm eighteen."

"*Eighteen!*" Now it was his turn to sound surprised, and she wished she had taken the chance of lying after all. "Did you say eighteen?"

"Efficiency is not always the product of experience," she hastened on. "And—and age was not stipulated in the advertisement."

"That's true." The amusement was back in his voice once more. "Very well, Miss Wood. I suggest you come for an interview. Would tomorrow be convenient for you?"

Julie was astounded. She was actually being granted an interview! She couldn't believe it.

"I asked if tomorrow would be convenient to you?"

The masculine voice sounded a little impatient now, and she hastened to assure him. "Tomorrow would be fine." Somehow it would have to be. She would have to think of some excuse to absent herself from the offices of Hollister, Barnes and Hollister, but she would do it.

"Then I suggest you come here—to the Limerick Hotel, at—let me see—one o'clock?"

"One o'clock!" That coincided with her lunch hour. She

might not have to think up excuses after all. "Er—who do I ask to see?"

"Oh yes—I forgot. The name is—Llewellyn, Rhys Llewellyn. Room 402."

Julie jotted it down swiftly. Rhys Llewellyn, Room 402. "I've got that. Thank you."

"Thank you, Miss Wood."

The line went dead, and Julie replaced her receiver with careful precision. Limerick Hotel, one o'clock, she repeated to herself. Rhys Llewellyn, Room 402.

She made sure the scrap of paper containing the information was safely in her handbag before her mother arrived home from the school fair. If she got the job, that would be time enough to tell her mother. And the chances of her doing so seemed remote indeed.

Nevertheless, she dressed with more than usual care the next morning, putting on the scarlet vinyl suit and matching boots she had treated herself to the previous week, and discarding her tweed coat for the belted raincoat which fell several inches below her knees. She had tried putting up her hair, but it didn't suit her, so she decided she would have to leave it loose after all. Even her mother forgot herself sufficiently to comment upon her appearance, and there was a speculative gleam in her eyes as she said:

"Don't tell me all this is for Mr. Hollister's benefit."

"It's not," replied Julie carelessly, seating herself at the kitchen table and tackling toast and marmalade, ignoring the calorie-conscious dictates of her conscience. "I just felt like getting dressed up for a change."

"Really?" Mrs. Wood sounded sceptical. "Just for a change, eh? And what time am I to expect you home this evening?"

"The usual time," answered Julie, finishing her toast and gulping hot coffee. She smiled at her mother's confusion. "See you later. Have a good day."

16

Several of the girls at the office made complimentary comments about her appearance, but she didn't rise to their baiting. Mr. Hollister seemed to find it difficult to take his eyes off her when she went in to take dictation, and she was glad to escape his covetous stare. Still, it was reassuring to know that she did look different, and as the clock crept round to lunch time she became more and more excited. Even if she didn't get the job, it was an adventure, something to add a little spice to her day.

The Limerick Hotel stood in a quiet square off Holborn, not too far from Hollister, Barnes and Hollister's offices in Gray's Inn. Julie had checked its whereabouts in the telephone directory the night before, and walked the distance easily in fifteen minutes. It was a small hotel, probably a very select establishment, she assured herself, after being disappointed that it wasn't anything like the Savoy or the Dorchester. An iron railing hid the basement from open view, and shallow steps gave on to a carpeted reception area. Julie mounted the steps, and approached the reception desk.

"My name is Wood. I have an appointment with Mr. Llewellyn for one o'clock," she announced herself quickly before nervousness made her turn tail and leave.

The receptionist looked up. She was exactly the sort of girl Julie had imagined getting this job, sleek and sophisticated, her smile faintly patronising.

"Miss—Wood?" She raised narrow eyebrows. "You have an appointment with Mr. Llewellyn?"

"Mr. Rhys Llewellyn. Yes," Julie pressed her lips together for a moment. "I rang yesterday evening."

"I'm afraid I wasn't on duty yesterday evening, Miss Wood, but if you'll wait a moment, I'll find out for you."

"Find out what?"

But Julie was being ignored, as the girl swung to her switchboard and began pressing buttons. Julie walked across the reception area, trying not to listen too consciously to what was being said, and was diverted by the arrival of an elderly man in a wheelchair, being hauled up the steps by a young man in chauffeur's uniform. The chauffeur eyed Julie with bold appraisal, and she swiftly looked away, not wanting to appear interested in him. But the sight of the wheelchair had given her an idea, and the chauffeur could quite easily have been the young man she had spoken to the night before.

"Miss Wood!"

The receptionist was calling her name as the chauffeur wheeled his charge into the lift, but it aroused no reaction and she walked rather dejectedly back to the desk.

"I'm afraid Mr. Llewellyn's associate can find no trace of your application, Miss Wood. All the interviews for the job were conducted this morning, I understand. I'm afraid you've made a mistake."

"The interviews were conducted this morning?" echoed Julie disbelievingly.

"Yes. Mr. Llewellyn wanted everything tying up with the least possible delay. I believe he is eager to return to his estate."

"His estate . . ."

Julie stared frustratedly at the immaculately groomed face of the girl across the desk, and a sense of anger and resentment grew inside her. So Mr. Llewellyn's associate didn't remember her? Or had the position been filled this morning and they had decided there was no point in seeing yet another unsuitable applicant? Julie felt tearful. It had all been a waste of time—coming here, raising her hopes. Oh, if she had the kind of courage they wrote about in books she would take the lift up to the fourth floor and tell Mr. Rhys Llewellyn and his associate exactly what she thought of them!

Her shoulders sagged. But she didn't have that kind of courage. Few people did. In fact, people didn't *do* that sort of thing at all. How could she march upstairs and demand an interview? What good would that do? They would probably have her thrown out, or arrested for assault or something. No stretch of her vivid imagination could see her accomplishing anything by such tactics.

"I'm sorry."

The receptionist was speaking again, and Julie shook her head. After all, it wasn't her fault. And she didn't look so supercilious now.

"Thank you anyway," she managed, and turned away, taking a deep breath and flinging her bag over her shoulder in a defiant gesture. Back to Hollister, Barnes and Hollister.

"Miss Wood! Julie!"

The voice was vaguely familiar, and Julie halted halfway down the steps and looked round to find a boy of not more than fourteen or fifteen rushing across the reception hall from the lift. Tall and thin, with bony humorous features half hidden behind horn-rimmed spectacles, casually dressed in jeans and a striped sweat shirt, he was no one's idea of a wealthy recluse, but Julie knew at once who he was.

"You're—you're the—person who spoke to me—on the phone last night!" she exclaimed.

He nodded, obviously out of breath, probably from hurrying. "That's right," he gulped. The voice was unmistakable. "Thank goodness I caught you! We don't even have your address."

Julie tried to remember her resentment of a few minutes before. "There's not much point in having my address, is there?" she countered impatiently. "I'm not even being granted an interview!" She frowned suddenly. "Are—are *you* Mr. Llewellyn's associate?"

"Me?" The boy laughed. "Hell, no!" He ignored her raised eyebrows and added: "Come on back inside. I want to talk to you, and it's too cold here."

Julie hesitated. "I've told you, there's no point . "

"There's every point. Please." He held out a hand. "Come into the lounge."

Julie looked up into his pale face, and the appeal in his dark eyes persuaded her. "All right," she agreed with some reluctance. "But I don't really see—"

"*William!* What in God's name do you think you're doing?"

As before, Julie was arrested by the sound of a voice, a voice not unlike the boy's, but with a deeper, almost lilting cadence, or it would have had had that quality not been overridden by the harshness of anger. A man had appeared behind the boy, a tall, lean man, whose dark features were presently drawn into grim lines. Dark brown hair, flecked with grey in places, grew low on his neck, and in sideburns almost to his jawline. He was not a handsome man, his features were too rugged for that, but there was something about their very harshness which gave them a certain rough attraction. He was a man in his late thirties, or possibly early forties, casually dressed like the boy, in tight-fitting black suede pants and a black, open-necked knitted sweater. Although the resemblance was slight, she guessed he could well be the boy's father.

William, if that was the boy's name, turned to the man with resignation, raking a hand through his untidy dark hair. "This is Miss Wood, Da. I told you I was going to speak to her."

"And I told you to stay in your room," retorted the man briefly.

Julie felt terrible. "Perhaps it would be as well if I left," she ventured uncomfortably, and the man nodded, his eyes coldly assessing.

"Perhaps it would," he agreed. "I'm sorry if you've been inconvenienced . . ."

"Couldn't you at least interview her, Da?" demanded the boy angrily. "I asked her to come here—"

"I appreciate that, William," returned the man with emphasis. "I apologise for my son's behaviour, Miss—Miss Wood?"

"That's all right." Julie found herself in the curious position of defending the boy. "I must have made a mistake—"

"There was no mistake!" asserted the boy, staring frustratedly at his father. He was breathing quickly again, as he had been when he first called to her, and patches of hectic colour were appearing in his cheeks. "Da, why can't you give her a chance? Talk to her at least. Her qualifications are excellent."

"You're upsetting yourself unnecessarily, William! And you're wasting Miss Wood's time."

"Oh, really, I—"

Julie's involuntary denial was ignored as William spoke only to his father: "Why are you so opposed to anyone I like? I've got to live with her, too, haven't I? Don't I get any say in the matter?"

"William, Mr. Thomas has got two perfectly suitable applicants to choose from. Let him decide."

"Oh, Mr. Thomas! That old fogey! It's you who wants the secretary, Da! Don't you care who you have working for you?"

"Not particularly."

The man's voice was coldly indifferent, and Julie shivered in spite of herself. If this man was the wealthy recluse, she was not at all sure she even wanted to be considered for the post. Not that she was being, really. This argument did not constitute a consideration. But she did like the look of William. And his behaviour was not so unusual for a boy of his age. She ought to have been angry with him. But it seemed as though he had enough anger going on around him as it was.

William was quite breathless now, and seemed to be having difficulty in breathing at all. Julie turned anxious eyes on his father, but that cold individual seemed indifferent to his son's predicament.

"I suggest we abandon this discussion before we are all arrested for causing a disturbance," he stated bleakly. "As I said before, Miss Wood, I'm sorry—"

"You're not sorry!" Julie heard herself saying with great trepidation. "You're just saying that. You don't mean it. Can't you see—your son is *ill*!"

There was a brief pregnant silence when all Julie could hear was William's tortured breathing, and the heavy pounding of her own heart. And then the man, who had been regarding her steadily for fully half a minute, indicated the swing doors to one side of the hall.

"I suggest we go in there," he said, in an ominously quiet tone, and without waiting for their compliance, he walked ahead of them into the elegantly furnished residents' lounge. There was something wrong with the way he walked, a certain stiffness in his gait which Julie found rather disturbing, but she had no time to ponder that right now as he stood by the open door, waiting for William and herself to join him.

With a helpless shrug at the boy, she walked through into the lounge, conscious that he was following her, turning to look apprehensively at his father. The man closed the door behind them, and then he said, in the same quiet tone: "Exactly what did my son tell you, Miss Wood?"

Julie licked her dry lips. "He—I—I rang last night and enquired about the advertisement in *The Times*, and he—he asked about my credentials."

"Indeed?" The man's lips twitched slightly. "And they are?"

Julie felt silly, but she had to answer him. "I—a hundred words a minute shorthand, seventy typing."

"Thank you." He turned to the boy. "Does that satisfy you?"

William had been using the time to regain his breath, but his face was still constricted with the effort, and perspiration beaded his forehead. Julie felt a wave of sympathy sweep over her just looking at him, and she turned stormy eyes on his father.

Who was this man? This Rhys Llewellyn? Had he no compassion?

William took a step forward. "Why—why can't we have someone—someone young?" he gasped painfully. "Someone I can talk to. Those—those other women, they're—they're old!"

"Thank you. They're younger than I am," retorted his father dryly. "William, I explained to you before. It's necessary that we have someone suitable." Then he looked back at Julie. "Why would a girl like you want to bury herself in the wilds of Cambria?"

CHAPTER TWO

Julie took a few seconds to absorb what he had said, and then she made an involuntary gesture. "The—the wilds of Cambbria?" She was confused, and disconcerted. "You mean—you mean *Wales*?"

She spoke the last word very faintly, and the man nodded with finality. "Yes, Miss Wood, Wales. Where else?"

Where indeed? "I—I—" Julie looked helplessly towards William, and intercepting her gaze the man's eyes narrowed comprehendingly.

"Ah!" he said, folding his arms across his broad chest. "I gather my son told you something else."

Julie was trying to think. Should she have suspected? The names – Rhys – Llewellyn – William, even. Should they have warned her? But why? These people could have lived anywhere. But obviously they didn't. This put an entirely different light on the situation. Would she even have considered the job if she had thought she was going to be asked to live in Wales? She knew nothing about the country. She had never been there and her impressions were of a wild and mountainous countryside, swept by rain and winds from the west.

Realising that they were both waiting for her to speak, she made an effort to behave normally. After all, William had never actually said where she might expect to live, except that the minimum of summer clothing would hardly do for Wales in winter.

"I—er—I'm surprised, that's all," she managed, shrugging her slim shoulders. "I mean—well, you don't sound Welsh," she finished lamely.

"Don't we?" A dark eyebrow quirked upward. "And our names are terribly Anglo-Saxon, of course."

"Llewellyn could have been an ancestral name."

"So it could. Perhaps I should have slipped in a couple of 'Look yous' and the odd 'Indeed to goodness', hmm?"

"Don't make fun of me!"

"It was my fault, Da," cried William, pushing his horn-rimmed spectacles further up his thin nose. "I told her she—"

"You didn't tell me anything!" Julie asserted sharply, her eyes flashing. "You didn't mention the location at all."

William's rueful grimace was grateful. "Thanks," he muttered gruffly, and she smiled sympathetically at him.

The corners of his father's mouth drew down. "What exactly did my son tell you, Miss Wood?"

Julie sighed, trying to remember. "I—not a lot. He asked the questions."

"And you were not sufficiently curious to ask questions yourself?"

"I—I—if you must know, I never expected to get an interview."

"Oh? Why not?"

Julie moved her shoulders helplessly. "Jobs like this are not thick on the ground."

"Jobs like what, Miss Wood?"

"Oh, stop pretending you don't understand what I'm trying to say! The advertisement sounded—fascinating, as I'm sure you realised. Anyone would jump at the chance!"

"Would they?" The man frowned. "It might interest you to know, Miss Wood, that out of twenty-seven applications, only two who met our requirements were prepared to accept the conditions of employment."

Julie's brow furrowed. "Only two?"

"Only two."

25

"But—" She glanced again at William. Had he lied about the salary, as well? "I—I thought the conditions of employment sounded quite—generous."

"A thousand a year, and your keep. Living in a remote coastal district of Wales. Without friends or contemporaries. It's not everyone's idea of generosity."

Julie caught her breath. *One* thousand a year – not two. And *Wales* – not the Bahamas. She might have known there was a catch somewhere.

She looked at William, and met his sheepish stare. He had good reason to look like that, she thought impatiently. Without his intervention, she would not be here. Nor would she be having this heated argument with a man whose attitude no longer seemed so unreasonable.

"Well, Miss Wood? You are now in possession of all the facts. Do you still want to be considered for the post?"

Julie gasped. "Am I being considered?"

"As you seem to regard me as some kind of monster, and William as an innocent babe in arms, I find myself inclined to disillusion you, Miss Wood."

"What do you mean?"

"I am not without experience of women, Miss Wood. I'm fully aware that my son must have painted a vastly different picture of the circumstances of this appointment than I have done. No doubt he tempted you with luxurious working conditions — a lucrative salary." His lips twisted. "I am not in the market for gold-diggers of that kind, Miss Wood."

Julie's lips parted indignantly. The fact that he was nearer the truth than even he might imagine did not matter. How dared he classify her on the strength of past experience?

"You haven't even told me what the work is yet," she retorted, not really knowing why she was going on with this. How could she even consider leaving her home and family, her

26

friends, to go and live in some cold and lonely outpost in Wales, being paid a salary that was less than she was earning now?

"My father's going to write a book!" exclaimed William eagerly, but was silenced by the look his father gave him. Nevertheless, Julie took it up.

"Is that true? Are you going to write a book, Mr. Llewellyn?"

The man's expression hardened. "And if I am?"

Julie lifted her shoulders in an eloquent little gesture. After months of typing legal documents, the idea of being involved in creative writing sounded inviting indeed.

"Am I to take it that in spite of all the disadvantages of the post, and I warn you there are many, you still want to be considered for the job?"

Llewellyn sounded bored by the whole proceeding, and she knew he was willing her to refuse. But something, some perverse desire to thwart this man who thought he knew all about girls like her, made her loath to back down. It was like admitting defeat. Of course, everyone would think she was mad, should the remote possibility of her being accepted occur. She could just imagine what Laura and her mother would say. And Mark, too. But it was an opportunity to escape from the future her mother was inexorably planning for her. Perhaps if she could convince her mother that she was determined to lead her own life, she would leave her alone. Mrs. Wood might even sell the house and go and live with Aunt Margaret in Southend as she wanted to do.

Taking a deep breath, she nodded her head and said: "Yes, Mr. Llewellyn, I think I should like to be considered."

"Hey—terrific!" William pressed balled fists together, but his father looked less enthusiastic.

"You realise you can't expect the modern conveniences you are used to, Miss Wood?" he commented dourly, pacing stiffly to the tall windows of the lounge. "The nearest town is fifteen miles away, and we have no television—"

"Oh, stop trying to put her off, Da!" exclaimed William fiercely, getting angry again. "Just because she's young and attractive! Just because I like her! Why shouldn't I have someone of my own age to talk to? You do!"

His father turned to face him, thick lashes narrowing eyes darkened by some emotion Julie could not identify. "William, if you had stayed in any one of the schools I selected for you, you'd have had dozens of people of your own age to talk to!" he stated grimly.

"Oh, yes." William's tone was bitter. "You'd have liked that, wouldn't you? You never wanted me, did you? You've made that transparently clear. And of course, Nerys doesn't want me either, does she? I get in the way. You don't give her enough attention when I'm around. Have you thought what she would say if you took someone like Miss Wood back to Devil's Mount?"

"That's enough, William!" His father's features were harsh with dislike. "A boy of your age should be in school!"

"*School!*" William's lips curled. "I hate schools!"

"Obviously, since you've succeeded in having yourself thrown out of three of them!"

Julie was beginning to feel uncomfortable again. This was a family quarrel, and she could see the telltale signs of breathlessness invading William's face again.

"If—if the interview is over—" she began awkwardly, but William turned to her beseechingly, reaching out a hand to stay her.

"Don't go! Please, Miss Wood, don't go! If you do, my father will appoint one of those other women, I know he will!" His breathing had quickened alarmingly, and he took great strangled gulps of air as he strove to go on speaking. "Your— your qualific—qualifications are as good as either of the

28

others." He turned to face his father. "Why can't we have— have her?"

Julie felt the boy's groping fingers fasten round her arm, and was filled with a half fearful sense of inevitability. Perceptively, she guessed that his father abhorred this show of weakness, but as William continued to gasp for breath beside her, desperation made her protest: "Is there nothing you can do for him?"

Rhys Llewellyn thrust his hands into the pockets of his pants, tautening the cloth across the powerful muscles of his thighs. Julie's eyes were drawn to him against her will. Something about this man disturbed her, adding to the conviction she could feel stirring inside her that she ought not to get involved with this family. What did she know of them, after all? What wealthy man, but an eccentric one, would live in the wilds of rural Wales? How could she be sure who they really were? What proof had she of their identity? None. And yet, unwillingly, she was involved, whether she liked it or not. Involved, because of a boy who had brought her here under false pretences, and who now revealed himself as more vulnerable than she was.

"I should explain that my son suffers from nervous asthma," Rhys Llewellyn said flatly, "but he is perfectly capable of inducing an attack should the situation warrant it."

Julie stared at him in disgust. "What a foul thing to suggest!"

"But honest," he retorted coldly. "My God, do you think I haven't seen this happen before? In fifteen years, I've had a few enlightening experiences with my son, and I can assure you his present condition is not unique!"

"You're—you're inhuman!" Julie tore her eyes away from him to stare unhappily at the boy. "How can you stand there and dismiss your own son so callously? Haven't you ever thought that he might have these attacks because of you?"

Rhys Llewellyn's next words did not bear repetition as he strode across the room and dragged William away from her. Putting his hands on his son's shoulders, he stared down at the boy intently, as though willing him to calm himself.

"All right, all right, William," he said through clenched teeth. "Miss Wood shall have the job, if she still wants it. But don't think you've fooled me—not for one minute." He released the boy so suddenly that he almost fell and turned back to Julie. "Well?"

He was much closer now, the dark eyes intent and intimidating. Julie's throat felt constricted, and her palms were moist. "I—well, what?" she faltered.

"Do you want the job or don't you?"

Julie moved awkwardly from one foot to the other, aware of the height and breadth of him, uneasily aware that if she committed herself to the boy she was committing herself to him too. "I—well, I have to discuss it with—with my family," she ventured.

Rhys Llewellyn's expression grew contemptuous. "I see. So your protestations on William's behalf were not as vehement as you would have me believe!"

"That's not true!" Julie's eyes shifted to the boy, noticing how tensely he was waiting for her reply. But already his breathing was easier. How could she risk upsetting him again? She spread her hands. "What do you expect me to say?" she implored.

"Say you'll take the job," answered William urgently. "Please!"

Rhys Llewellyn was watching her equally closely, and when she looked up into his dark Celtic features she was not surprised to see the scornful twist to his mouth.

"Well, Miss Wood?" he mocked.

Julie combed her fingers through the straight curtain of her hair. "I—I—"

"You have no choice, do you?" he asked sardonically. "A powerful weapon, you must agree."

"It's not like that," she cried, looking away from him.

"Isn't it?" He didn't sound convinced. "Very well, Miss Wood. Are you accepting the post?"

Julie looked down at her hands, then at William, and finally at Rhys Llewellyn once more. "I—yes. Yes. But I have to give notice at my present place of employment."

"Which is?"

"A solicitor's office. Hollister, Barnes and Hollister."

"That means nothing to me." Rhys Llewellyn was taking a notepad out of his back pocket. "Okay," he wrote something down, "this is my address. If you cable us the date and time of your arrival, I'll arrange for you to be met at Fishguard. How much notice will you have to give?"

"Two weeks—I think."

"Two weeks!" William sounded dismayed. "Can't you make it one?"

Rhys Llewellyn tore a sheet off his pad and handed it to Julie, and her eyes scanned the words *Devil's Mount* and *Abernarth* before he spoke again.

"Should you require any further particulars, you can contact me through my solicitors – Latimer, Leazes, Thomas and Lane."

Julie caught her lower lip between her teeth. "But don't you want to test me? Check that I'm not lying about my typing and shorthand speeds?"

Rhys Llewellyn regarded her unemotionally. "Are you lying?"

"*No!*"

"I'll accept that. I shouldn't like to be in your shoes if you come to Devil's Mount under false pretences," he remarked dryly.

"You're trying to frighten her!" declared William angrily.

31

"You won't change your mind, will you?" This to Julie.

Julie shook her head helplessly. "You don't even know my address!"

Rhys Llewellyn opened his note book again. "If it will make you any happier, you can give it to me," he said resignedly.

Julie pursed her lips. Then she said: "Thirty-six, Eastman Road, Romford," rather resentfully.

"Fine." He straightened, flinching as a spasm of pain crossed his face. But the emotion she glimpsed was so fleeting, she half thought afterwards that she had imagined it. "That concludes the negotiation, I think." His lips twitched with faint amusement. "I hope you won't live to regret your decision, Miss Wood."

Julie hoped so, too, and as she walked back to Gray's Inn, her thoughts tumbled madly round inside her head. What had she done? she asked herself confusedly. Committing herself without even taking the time to reconsider. What was her mother going to say? Giving up a perfectly good job in the city to go and live in such an outlandish place! And for less money! She must have been mad even to consider it! But consider it she had, and there seemed no way of backing out of it.

She blinked rapidly. Away from William's distressed presence, it was difficult to understand why she had not simply turned him down flat. Obviously, his father knew him better than she did, and their private affairs were not her concern. Yet she had made them so—to the extent that she had become personally involved in their family conflict.

And then there was Rhys Llewellyn himself, her new employer. What manner of man was he really? Why did he walk so stiffly? Was that pain she had seen in his face? And why did she feel this disturbing awareness of him, that was at once magnetic and repelling? She had the feeling she was stepping out of her depth, into waters both deep and unknown, full of tides and currents that as yet she had barely touched upon. She recalled the name of someone called Nerys. Who was that? Her employer's wife? But not William's mother, that much seemed certain. Why hadn't she asked more questions? Discovered who else lived at Devil's Mount? Asked in what capacity she was to live there? She knew nothing about living in someone else's house as their employee. Her parents had never had employees, of any kind, and her knowledge was limited to what she had gleaned from historical novels and the like. What if she didn't like the work? What if she was unhappy there? Abernarth was a long way from Eastman Road—and even further from Southend . . .

She was late back to the office, and Mr. Hollister had already sent for her. When she shed her coat and made her way to his office, still in the slightly dazed condition in which she had left the Limerick Hotel, she found him in a vastly less amiable frame of mind than he had been in that morning.

"Are you aware it's now almost half past two?" he demanded, pacing furiously about his office, puffing on the inevitable cigar which was to be found in his mouth. Short and tubby, he had always reminded Julie of Toad of Toad Hall, but today reality had less conviction about it than fiction.

Gathering herself with difficulty, Julie began to apologise, and then, realising that now was as good a time as any to tell him of her proposed change in circumstances, she said: "I'd like you to accept my resignation, Mr. Hollister."

Her words halted his restless meanderings, and he stopped to stare at her, taking the cigar out of his mouth. "What did you say?"

"I'm giving you two weeks' notice, Mr. Hollister. That is what's required, isn't it?"

"Two weeks' notice?" Hector Hollister pulled out a red spotted handkerchief, and looking more and more like Kenneth Grahame's prodigy, began to bluster: "Now look here, Julie, I know I'm not a patient man at the best of times, and maybe I

33

have been a little hard on you lately, but that's no reason for you to say you're leaving us! Good heavens, I know I probably seem old-fashioned to you, demanding punctuality, that sort of thing, but dammit, I am your employer!"

"I know that, Mr. Hollister." Julie was astonished at this display, and a little embarrassed, too.

"Well," Hector Hollister mopped his brow, "of course, I guessed you'd got something on today, all dressed up like that. New boy-friend, is it? And why not? Wish I was ten years younger. I'd be after you myself."

"Mr. Hollister, it—"

"No need to be hasty, Julie. That's what I always say. You're a damn good secretary, that's what you are, damn good! Don't want to lose you. Can't say fairer than that."

"Mr. Hollister, I'm not leaving because—well, because of you. I've got another job. I went for an interview at lunchtime. That's why I was late."

Hector sank down weakly into the chair behind his desk. "You've got another job?" he echoed. "Where? In London?"

"Actually, no. It's not in London at all. I—er—I felt like a change of scenery. It's in Wales. I'm going to work for a—a writer."

"Who is it? Do I know him?"

"I—I shouldn't think so."

Julie was loath to mention Rhys Llewellyn's name, but Hector was not about to allow her to get away with it so easily.

"Don't you need a reference?" he enquired curiously, looking up at her through a veil of cigar smoke. His thick lips curled. "Or aren't you going to be his—secretary?"

Julie stiffened. "There's no need to be offensive, Mr. Hollister. And I don't recall actually saying that my new employer was male!"

Hector sighed, shaking his head. "Nor you did. But they usually are—those who employ secretaries, I mean." He pres-

34

sed out the stub of his cigar in the ashtray, and when next he looked at her there was resignation in his gaze. "I'm sorry, Julie. But you've really taken me unawares. Put it down to my regret at losing you."

Julie had never heard Hector Hollister apologise to anyone before, and his manner disarmed her. "As a matter of fact, you're right," she admitted quietly. "My new employer is a man. His name—his name is Rhys—Llewellyn."

Hector's heavy brows met above the bridge of his nose. "Llewellyn? Did you say Llewellyn?"

Julie's nails curled into her palms. "Yes. Why? Do you know him?"

"Rhys Llewellyn? No. But I do know of a Rhys Edwards who has recently returned to live in Wales."

"I expect Rhys is a common enough name there."

"Perhaps so." Hector leaned back in his chair. "And this man I'm thinking about is no suitable employer for an attractive young girl like you."

Considering his own sometimes less than proper behaviour, Julie had to smile. But she asked him what he meant all the same.

Hector pulled a face. "No need to go into details. The man's an ex-mercenary. Dangerous type. Inherited a great deal of money and land through the death of his elder brother. Completely without scruple, so I hear. Didn't you read anything about it in the papers? His brother was killed in that plane crash six months ago in France. He was the Marquis of Llantreath or something like that. I suppose that makes Edwards the Marquis now. What irony! I understand the brothers hated one another. He'd have some story to write!"

Julie could feel a curious prickling sensation along her spine. "Is he—was he ever married?" she asked, with what she hoped was casual interest. "Does he—have any children?"

"Who? Edwards or his brother?"

35

"I—well, Edwards, I suppose."

"Not so far as I know. But I mean, I don't know the whole story. Only what I read in the papers and what I pick up among my colleagues in the profession. I think the Marquis— the dead brother, that is—was married, but I'm not even sure of that."

Julie nodded. Oh, well, she thought with relief, that seemed reassuring. And in any case, why should she imagine that this man Mr. Hollister was gossiping about could have any connection with the Rhys Llewellyn she was to work for? But it was a coincidence, just the same, and she couldn't help thinking about it as she travelled home on the train that evening. It distracted her thoughts from the prospect of facing her mother.

She could imagine Rhys Llewellyn as a mercenary, she thought broodingly. He was just as hard and callous as she would imagine them to be, and unwillingly she thought of her Viking. What had he been, after all, but a mercenary, raping and pillaging, his sword stained brightly with the blood of his victims? But Rhys Llewellyn was nothing like the golden-haired hero of her fantasies. Big and powerful he might be, cruel and ruthless even, but without that gentle side to his nature which could disarm the most defiant maiden and seduce her into yielding compliance in his arms ...

CHAPTER THREE

THE train ran into Goodwick station in the late afternoon. Darkness was already deepening beyond the misted windows of the compartment, and the encroaching night made the circumstances of her arrival that much more nerve-racking somehow. The journey had been long and uneventful, giving Julie plenty of time to brood about this step she was taking, and she continually asked herself what she was doing here. But she had no answer to give.

The last two weeks had not helped. Far from being pleased that she was leaving home, her mother had adopted a martyred air, and had veered from tearful anxiety about Julie's future to what the neighbours would say when they found out. Julie guessed her departure would arouse some speculation, not least being the speed with which it was to be accomplished, and her mother would not relish explaining where she had gone. It had all been most upsetting for Julie, who herself was unconvinced that she was doing the right thing. There were times when she found herself actually composing letters of apology to Rhys Llewellyn, explaining that she could not take the position after all, but then she thought about William and tore them up.

Mark, who she had expected to be angry, had shown a surprising amount of understanding, and perversely this had not helped. Why couldn't she have been like Laura? she had asked herself over and over again. Why couldn't she have been content to marry Mark, who was a good man, and periodically produce his children? Why couldn't she have liked knitting and baking and joining Young Wives' clubs, sharing in the

37

social life of a new housing estate? How could she and her sister be so completely different from one another?

And the chilling thought had remained that perhaps they were not so different, after all. Perhaps Laura had curbed this restless impulse that surged so strongly in Julie to look for more in life than was offered in their narrow little circle. Perhaps she had more sense than to go seeking the unknown. Who in their right minds would leave a secure and comfortable environment for the wilds of Wales in winter, working for a man whose character was, to say the least, suspect, and whose relationship with his son bordered on the barbaric?

The railway station was reassuringly normal, with passengers disgorging from the train, tugging out their luggage, fumbling for their tickets, their breath clouding in the cold air. Julie pulled out her own two cases and searched in her bag for the square of cardboard which entitled her to travel. The wind made an eerie sound as it whistled down the draughty tunnel of the platform, and she was glad she had chosen to wear warm trousers and a chunky sweater under her tweed coat.

She had cabled the date and time of her arrival to Rhys Llewellyn as he had directed, and as she lugged her cases towards the barrier, she looked round hopefully for a familiar face. But although everyone else linked up with friends or relatives, or disappeared about their own business, Julie emerged from the station without encountering anyone who appeared to be looking for her.

She sighed. This was the last straw! The least they could have done was be on time to meet her, particularly as it was so cold, and the mist which swept round her and smelled of the sea chilled her to the bone. She couldn't walk far even if she had wanted to, with her cases, and she thought with nostalgia of her departure from London, with her mother and Laura, and Laura's husband, Alan, all waiting to see her off. Alan had carried her cases to the train, and she had reassured herself that someone else would be there to carry them at the other end. But instead, she seemed to have been abandoned, and it was difficult to control the sense of tearful resentment which filled her.

After waiting fifteen minutes, she struggled her cases back to the ticket office.

"Excuse me," she asked the operator politely, "but is there another train from London tonight?"

The girl behind the counter shook her head. "No."

Julie digested this with dismay. "There isn't?"

"No. The London train came in nearly half an hour ago."

"I know that. I was on it." Julie countered the girl's curious stare. "I was supposed to have someone meeting me. They haven't arrived."

"Oh. There's a pity."

"Yes. Isn't there?" Julie spoke distractedly, and then realising what she was saying, amended: "Isn't it?"

"And do you have far to go?" At least someone was not indifferent to her plight.

"A place called—Abernarth."

"Abernarth?" The girl rubbed her nose. "Ah."

"Is it far?"

"Oh—twenty-five miles, at least—"

"Twenty-eight, actually."

The hard masculine tones were unmistakably familiar, and Julie turned with mixed feelings of apprehension and relief to find Rhys Llewellyn standing right behind her. In a fur-collared black leather coat over equally dark pants, thick dark hair lifting in the draught, his tanned features glowing with health in the sharp air, he looked disturbingly attractive, and Julie would have been inhuman not to be aware of it. The girl behind the ticket counter obviously was, her attitude melting beneath his undoubted sex appeal, her eyes betraying a message that even Julie understood.

"Do you live in Abernarth?" she asked him, and Rhys Llewellyn nodded his head.

"Near enough," he conceded lightly. "Can I be of some assistance?"

Julie's lips parted on a gasp at his words, and when the girl began to explain how this passenger had expected to be met from the London train and was now stranded twenty-eight miles from her destination, she stared at him angrily, waiting for him to cut her off. But he didn't. He merely revealed a polite interest in her predicament, and then had the nerve to offer her a lift.

"I'm driving back to Abernarth this evening," he remarked, with cool insolence. "I'd be happy to see you to your destination."

Julie stared at him for a few moments longer, but she could not sustain the mocking challenge in those dark eyes, and with a defeated little exclamation, she swung about and marched away determinedly towards the exit. She was aware that the girl behind the ticket counter was staring after her disbelievingly, probably considering her mad to apparently reject such an attractive offer, but the man was impossible, and right now she was in no state to deal with him. How could he stand there and behave as if he'd never set eyes on her before? He was just as objectionable as she had imagined.

"I imagine you'll be needing these."

She had halted outside the station, and when her tormentor's voice spoke close to her ear, she looked up to find him holding one of her cases in each hand. Realising she had left them standing by the ticket office, she roused a reluctant consent.

"Yes." A pause. "Thank you."

He looked down at her half impatiently. "What's wrong?"

Indignation exploded into anger. "You ask me that!"

He glanced all about them, and then nodded. "It would seem

like it.''

"Oh—oh, you're so sarcastic, aren't you? And so clever!''

"Am I?'' He raised a dark eyebrow. "Well, considering how little you know of me, I consider that a perceptive statement. Thank you.''

Julie pressed her lips together, staring at him impotently, and he put down one of the cases to gesture towards a mud-smeared station wagon parked a little distance away.

"Let's continue this fascinating conversation in the car, shall we? I don't know what you've got in these cases, but it feels like chain mail!''

Julie had no choice but to follow him across to the station wagon, waiting while he stowed her cases in the back before holding open the door for her to climb inside. Then he walked round the bonnet to slide in beside her, his thigh brushing hers as he made himself comfortable. He inserted his key in the ignition, but before starting the engine, he looked sideways at her.

"Now—let's hear it, shall we?''

Julie took a deep breath. "You know perfectly well what I'm going to say! Why did you pretend you'd never seen me before? Making a fool of me in front of that girl in the ticket office!''

"How did I do that?'' His eyes were mocking. "She wasn't to know we were old friends.''

"We are not old friends!''

"No. Well, perhaps that was an unfortunate choice of phrase. Nevertheless, until you stormed off, it seemed a perfectly natural situation to her.''

"Oh, yes.'' Julie's tone was bitter. "I'm quite sure *she* wouldn't have quibbled about being in my position!''

His smile was infuriatingly complacent. "I had the same impression,'' he remarked, without conceit.

Julie uttered a frustrated sound. "The least you could have

done was be here on time! I've been waiting almost half an hour!"

"Ah!" He rubbed the side of his nose. "Well, there was a reason for that."

"A puncture, no doubt!"

Julie was amazed at her own temerity, but his behaviour had not exactly been responsible either. With a slight, indifferent shrug of his leather-clad shoulders, he seemed to concede the point however, and swinging round in his seat flicked the ignition. The powerful engine roared into life, and he reversed with evident expertise out of the parking area. Julie sat stiffly, half prepared for him to make some scathing retort, but nothing was forthcoming, and she was compelled to an uneasy silence.

Street lamps were lighted, casting pools of shadow beyond their circles of light. Mist hazed the windscreen both inside and out, as warm breath encountered cold glass, and Julie was glad of the car's heater to warm her booted toes. She had little idea of the direction he might be taking, and wondered if the poor weather conditions had anything to do with his being late. If that were so, perhaps she owed him an apology. But why should she apologise? she argued with herself. He hadn't!

The car smelt pleasantly of leather and tobacco—not cigarette tobacco, but something cleaner, rather a nice smell, she decided. It was incredibly untidy, with scraps of paper and old magazines stuffed into the flaps in the door and down between the seats. A heavy, rubber-bound torch and a roll of string resided on the parcel shelf, and two empty beer cans nudged her feet. It was nothing like the Rolls she might have expected a wealthy man to favour, and she wondered again whether she had been mad to accept him on trust.

The lights of shop windows were reassuringly distracting, and noticing her attention, her companion spoke again. "This is Fishguard," he remarked lazily. "Did you know? And al-

42

though you can't see anything this evening, there's quite a view over the Bay from this headland. Down below us is what they call Lower Fishguard. Have you heard of it?" Julie shook her head, and he went on: "I thought you might have done. It's the old port. They filmed Dylan Thomas's *Under Milk Wood* there. Richard Burton stirred a few hearts, so I've heard."

Julie was intrigued in spite of herself. "I didn't know."

"No. Well, perhaps you are a bit young at that."

Julie let that go, and he glanced her way again.

"Aren't you going to tell me how old you are?" he enquired mockingly. "Young women usually do, and older women usually don't."

"And you've known both, I suppose!"

"In my time," he conceded lightly. "You're a prickly little thing, aren't you, Miss Wood? I had thought it was all to do with your feelings over my son, but I'm beginning to think he was only an excuse."

Julie sighed, realising the truth in what he said. But still she couldn't allow him to get away with all of it. "You seem to be forgetting the fact that all this is strange to me. Leaving home, coming here—waiting hours on the station!"

"Hours, is it?" All of a sudden he sounded very Welsh, and she liked it. "I was twenty-nine minutes late at the very most. And had it not been for William throwing an attack before I left, I would have been here before you."

"William?" She turned to him. "He had an attack? But why?"

"He wanted to come with me to meet you, why else?"

"And you wouldn't let him?"

"No, I wouldn't let him."

Julie's nails curled into her palms. "Surely you could have permitted him to come along?" she exclaimed. "What possible objection could you have to that?"

Rhys Llewellyn's profile had hardened. "I don't have to

43

explain my actions to you, Miss Wood."

"No, you don't." Julie swung round in her seat now. "But I think you're unnecessarily harsh with the boy."

"I'd gathered that. However, as he's just recovering from a severe attack of bronchitis, I hardly consider driving fifty-odd miles in these conditions a suitable method of recuperation."

Julie caught her breath. "Oh!"

"As you say—*oh!*"

Julie sighed. "I—I'm sorry. I—I didn't know."

"How could you? Nevertheless, I would suggest you endeavour to keep your opinions objective until you know all the facts."

Julie brushed back a strand of silky hair from her forehead. The lights of the town had been left behind them now and darkness was closing in around them, only the headlights of this car and others they passed illuminating the road ahead.

"So—so how is he, then?" she managed, into the silence that had fallen.

"As I've said—he's recovering. He's tougher than you give him credit for."

Julie bent her head. "His attacks are—frightening, though, aren't they?"

"They're distressing. Possibly more distressing for the onlooker than for William himself."

"Do you believe that?"

"I know it." His voice had hardened again. "And the headmasters of three public schools know it, too."

Julie sighed. "Is there nothing can be done for him?"

"Yes. He can receive a little less attention than he has been doing. Only time and determination will defeat him."

"That sounds awfully hard. What—what does your wife say?"

"My wife?" He sounded amused. "I have no wife."

"You don't?" Julie stared at him in the darkness. "But—"

"—I have a son, is that it?"

Julie turned to look out of the window at the hedges rushing past. All of a sudden, she didn't want to know. But it was too late.

"Oh, come, Miss Wood," he mocked. "You belong to this liberated generation growing up in Britain at the moment. Surely you don't believe that two people need to be married to produce a child!" She did not reply, and he expelled his breath impatiently. "I'm sorry if I've offended your sensibilities, but it seems to me, Miss Wood, you've been living a singularly narrow existence. Life is not all like the plastic world inside the cathode tube. Real people don't conform to any particular pattern. They have doubts—and failings some more than others."

Julie's fingers were entwined in the strap of her handbag. "I—it's nothing to do with me," she said stiffly.

"Isn't it?" His tone was vaguely bitter. "But you are going to be living in my house, aren't you? And I don't want to see those reproachful eyes of yours following me about. Yes, I knew we should have had someone older!"

"Why?" Julie was indignant. "People's attitudes don't always broaden with age."

"No," he agreed consideringly. "You're right, of course. Some are bigots all their lives."

"I'm not a bigot!"

"Aren't you? But you're shocked because William's a—"

"Don't say it!"

Impulsively, she stretched out her hand and touched his knee, intending to silence him. But when her fingers encountered the hard muscle of his thigh, they withdrew again with instinctive recoil. Her action brought his eyes to her again, enigmatic in the shadowy light emanating from the dash.

"What's wrong, Miss Wood? Have you never touched a man's knee before?"

"I—yes. Yes, of course I have."

"Really? So why did you draw back just now as if you'd burned yourself?"

"I'm—I'm not in the habit of touching strange men, Mr. Llewellyn."

"I'll bet you're not!" His laugh was faintly derisory. "I just wonder how an innocent like you was allowed to leave home."

Julie pursed her lips. "Nobody—allowed me. I make my own decisions, Mr Llewellyn. I'm not a child. And just because I don't find illegitimacy particularly amusing it's no reason for you to make fun of me!"

"I don't find illegitimacy amusing either," he retorted, his tone roughening. "But there are worse things, believe me!"

Julie heard the conviction in his voice and wondered what had happened to make him so cynical. What manner of man was he? What kind of life had he led to speak so convincingly of the darker side of human nature? Of what use had his money been to him?

She stared out into the darkness. For some time now they had been steadily ascending into the mountains, and the road was practically deserted. The mist was sparser up here, and through it she glimpsed the lights of a distant farmhouse. How much further had they to go? How much longer before they reached the comparative security of his house?

As though sensing her troubled thoughts, he suddenly spoke again, less aggressively now. "Are you hungry? I'm sorry, it's after six. But I never gave it a thought."

Julie glanced his way. "Is—is it much further?"

"About ten miles. If it hadn't been such a foul night, you'd have been able to see the lights of Cardigan Bay below us. But Abernarth is only a small fishing community, and Devil's Mount stands on the cliffs about a mile and a half from the village."

Julie nodded. "I'm looking forward to seeing it." And,

lyn had overtaken her again, and noticing her
ʒe said: "My sister-in-law, Nerys. Come and
d Dulcie."

nued on up the steps, but her feet were not so
She was recalling what William had said about
lled Nerys, about how she did not want him, how
the way when she was around. What had he meant?
erys had to be Rhys Llewellyn's brother's wife. So
s she here—at Devil's Mount? Unless his brother
ere, too. There was something about these thoughts
troubled her, something she vaguely remembered some-
ying . . .

ey had reached the porch at the top of the steps, and
s Llewellyn set down her cases with evident relief. The
d, Dulcie, danced about his long legs, begging to be picked
. Julie estimated that she was not more than five or six, and
om her behaviour she guessed she was used to getting her
own way.

But just at the moment, Rhys was more concerned with in-
troducing Julie to his sister-in-law. Nerys Llewellyn had said
nothing as yet, but her eyes rested frequently on her brother-
in-law's dark face, and there was in those eyes a look which
even Julie could not mistake. For once, it seemed, William
had not been exaggerating. Nerys Llewellyn was involved with
her brother-in-law, but whether he was involved with her
was another matter.

"This is Miss Wood, Nerys," Rhys was saying, somewhat
wearily. "Miss Wood—my sister-in-law, Mrs—Llewellyn."

"Llewellyn-Edwards," corrected Nerys smoothly, arousing
an impatient declaimer from her husband's brother. "How do
you do, Miss Wood? Should I say, welcome to Devil's Mount?
For once William was telling the truth. You are—more his age
than ours, aren't you?"

The words were spoken with deliberate intent, and Julie had

amazingly, she was.

"Are you?" His response was less enthusiastic. He sighed.
"There's a pub hereabouts where we can get a sandwich, if you
like."

Julie shook her head. "I'm not worried if you're not." She
paused. "Is there—is there anyone else living at—at Devil's
Mount, besides William and yourself?"

The words came out with a rush and she saw the downward
curve of his lips. "Three other adults, as a matter of fact," he
stated expressionlessly.

"Oh!"

"Aren't you going to ask who they are?"

"I—it's not my place to do so."

"Your place!" He uttered an impatient oath. "Then let's
hope you remember to keep to *your place*, Miss Wood."

The remainder of the journey was completed in silence, and
Julie had plenty of time to ponder his strange shifts of mood.
She did not understand him, but then she supposed she could
hardly expect to do so on such short acquaintance. And yet he
intrigued her. She had never met anyone quite like him before,
and she realised she found their verbal sparring stimulating.
He was as different from the young men she had known all her
life as the jungle animal was different from its domestic
counterpart, and Mark Roberts was a boy in comparison. She
had never been so aware of a man before, aware of his body as
well as his mind, and Rhys Llewellyn's age was no barrier to
his undoubted sensuality. Trying to rationalise her feelings
towards him was an impossible task for one so unsophisticated,
but common sense warned her that such a combination was
dangerous. It was as well he was too old for her, that he considered her a child. She had no wish to find herself in the kind
of position William's mother must once have experienced.

The mist was lifting as they came down the winding slope
into Abernarth. The road ran for some distance beside the sea,

passing a small harbour where boats bobbed at the jetty and a group of fishermen gathered together talking. They raised their heads as the car went by, but none of them acknowledged the man beside her, and he said nothing. Whitewashed cottages which would look picturesque on a summer's afternoon huddled about a small cobbled square, and the steeple of a chapel appeared above smoking chimneys. A smell of salt invaded the car for a period and then they had turned between the cottages, following the steep incline up towards the cliffs.

Devil's Mount stood on a headland, with the sea on two sides and a rocky promontory on the third. They approached along the coast road, swinging between rusting iron gates and traversing a drive which only the drifting leaves of autumn had saved from looking derelict. The house itself was square and ugly, dark brick, in places covered in moss and creeper, with long, narrow windows reminiscent of a fortress. As Rhys Llewellyn brought the station wagon to a halt at the foot of elaborately sculpted stone steps, which curved in two halves to a small balcony before becoming a single flight leading up to the doors of the house, Julie thrust open the door and climbed out. The thunderous roar of the sea was muted here, but she guessed there was no part of Devil's Mount free from the sound of its continuous motion. The air was sharp and cold, but not frosty, and overhead the clouds had rolled away to reveal a pale moon riding low in the sky. She breathed deeply, conscious of a feeling of wellbeing, that was quickly dispelled by the sound of Rhys Llewellyn hefting her cases out of the station wagon. Nevertheless, she could not deny the sense of excitement which filled her. Whatever else this position lacked, she was convinced her life here would not be dull.

Her new employer picked up her cases and indicated the steps. "Go ahead," he said. "I'll follow."

Julie hesitated. Surely he could have left her cases for one of the servants? A house this size must have servants, she

thought impatiently. But [...] self, and if he chose [...] the steps, who was she [...]

Before they were half [...] door above them opened, [...] illuminate their progress. L[...] jumping about excitedly at t[...] "Uncle Rhys! Uncle Rhys! You [...] treble.

Julie looked over her shoulder at [...] felt a reluctant sense of anxiety at the l[...] He looked positively haggard, and the sm[...] the child's benefit was a mere travesty. Un[...] led that day in the hotel in London. She had [...] awkwardly, stiffly, then. Obviously he had ha[...] with his back to find carrying two suitcases su[...] ordeal.

With a feeling of embarrassment, she halted a[...] for him to reach her before saying: "Let me take [...] those," but he shook his head, his expression dark[...] angrily.

"I can manage," he retorted, through thin lips. "I'm n[...] quite useless!"

"I never thought you were."

Julie moved her shoulders dismissingly, and hastened on up the steps. Then she hesitated again. The little girl had now been joined by a woman, a small slender individual, with a mass of curly ash-fair hair and delicately moulded features. Her ankle-length gown of dark blue wool was edged with multi-coloured braid, and its simplicity was clearly deliberate and exclusive. Whoever she was, and Julie guessed from the resemblance that she was the child's mother, she was no servant, and her appearance was the first outward sign of indulgence she had seen.

to bite back her indignation. Fortunately perhaps, at that moment, Dulcie grew tired of being ignored and set up a sulky wailing, and as Rhys bent to lift the child into his arms, another man appeared behind Nerys. He was not a young man, at least sixty, Julie surmised, with a shock of grey hair and bushy eyebrows. But he walked without any sign of a stoop, and lifted her cases without apparent effort.

"You'd all better come inside," he said, with the lilting accent of his ancestors. "How can I keep the place warm with doors standing open on a night like this?"

His actions promoted a general move inside the heavy doors of the building, and Julie looked about her with curious interest. The light which had illuminated the steps before the older man closed the door behind them came from a chandelier suspended incongruously above a hall that was sadly lacking in either design or comfort. Dust smudged the wood-blocked floor, revealing fingermarks on an enormous ebony chest. There was room for an ugly old-fashioned sideboard at the foot of stairs which ran along two walls of the hall and formed a balcony above the others. A single runner of carpet crossed the hall and followed the line of the stairs, its faded pattern eloquent of the atmosphere Julie could sense with a feeling of dismay. No one cared about this place, she thought almost sadly, and like an ugly woman it had lost its sparkle.

Her eyes shifted to Rhys Llewellyn, who was pacifying the little girl with a bar of candy taken from his pocket. Julie, who suspected Dulcie required a little more of the treatment he reserved for his son, felt a curious sense of displeasure watching the child in his arms, but Nerys was obviously well pleased, keeping close beside them, her eyes lingering deliberately on Julie as she whispered softly in Rhys's ear.

"Will I show the young lady to her room, Mr. Edwards?"

The older man had spoken, and Rhys set the child firmly on

her feet again before straightening to introduce his new secretary. But Julie was not paying any attention — not to Dulcie, who was complaining bitterly that Uncle Rhys didn't love her any more, nor to her mother, who was comforting her with assurances that she was still his little sweetheart, nor even to Rhys himself as he told her the man's name. She was back in Hector Hollister's office, and he was telling her about a Welshman who had returned home on the death of his elder brother, an elder brother whom he had thought to have been married! Rhys *Edwards* – she remembered the name distinctly, an ex-mercenary, who had inherited his brother's lands and his title. And that was the name Nerys had added to her name, too, only she hadn't given it a thought at the time. But now . . . Did that account for that curious feeling of identity she had experienced since getting out of the car?

"Miss Wood!"

Her own name, spoken with asperity, brought her head up sharply, but she could not entirely hide the startled awareness of her eyes. Yes, this might well be the Rhys Edwards Mr. Hollister had spoken of. Those lines of toughness and harsh cynicism in his face had not been etched by a gentle existence, that ruthless quality about him came from years of fighting for what he wanted, without giving or demanding any favours from anyone.

His eyes narrowed as he looked at her, and for a heart-stopping moment she thought he had guessed what she was thinking and intended taking her up on it. But instead, he indicated the older man. "Haggar will take you up to your room," he stated expressionlessly. "I've told him you haven't eaten, and instructed that you should have something brought to your room. I expect you're tired after your journey, so we won't enforce your company this evening. However, breakfast is at eight in the morning, and I shall expect you to be ready for work by nine. Is that understood?"

Julie nodded. She could have protested that he had not told her his real name, that to a certain extent he had brought her here under false pretences. But she remained silent, conscious, as Nerys watched her with faintly scornful eyes, that he was treating her as his employee for the first time. And she couldn't honestly say she liked the experience.

Haggar was walking towards the stairs, and she was following him, when a door to the right of the hall was wrenched open, emitting a draught of warm air into the decidedly chilly reaches of the entrance. William's thin, ungainly body appeared in the aperture, his face flushed and hectic-striped pyjama trouser legs showing below his grey woollen dressing gown. Julie was surprised at the relief she felt upon seeing him, but her reactions were tepid compared to the boy's.

"Julie! Julie," he exclaimed, and then after a salutory remonstrance from his father: "I mean—Miss Wood!" He spread his hands. "I didn't hear the car!" He opened the door invitingly wider, and Julie could see the reflection of flames from a fire leaping up the walls. "What are you doing out here? Come on in! I've been waiting for you."

Before Julie could speak, his father had crossed the hall and was propelling his son back into the warm room.

"Stay inside, William!" she heard Rhys say impatiently. "You're not even supposed to be out of bed! Doctor Matthews will lynch me if he finds out you've been wandering about draughty hallways in your condition."

"But I want to see Julie—"

Julie heard his protests before the door was kicked to behind them, and Dulcie set up her own shrill objections.

"Why has Uncle Rhys closed the door, Mummy? Why has he shut us out? I want to go in there, too. Uncle Rhys likes me, not that silly Willie!"

She darted across the hall to the room where the murmur of voices could still be heard, but as Haggar was already standing on the first landing waiting for her, Julie had no choice but to follow him upstairs. She was aware that Nerys crossed the hall after her daughter, and presently the door opened and closed behind both of them.

CHAPTER FOUR

JULIE'S room was at the back of the house, facing the deep channel which separated Wales from southern Ireland. It was an enormous apartment, with a high, moulded ceiling and bare, colourwashed walls. A marble-topped washstand was flanked on one side by a huge tallboy, and by a wardrobe big enough to store a dozen bodies on the other. The bed was four-posted, strong and square, its faded bedspread matching an equally faded canopy. But the sheets were very clean, and when she slid between them later that evening, she found a stone water bottle to warm her feet. There was a fireplace, and someone had thought to light a small fire in the grate, and this more than anything gave the room a welcoming appearance.

Waking in the morning to the sound of the waves breaking on the rocks below Devil's Mount, Julie lay for several min-utes absorbing the strangeness of her surroundings. The night before, she had found sleep a welcome escape from her thoughts, but this morning her brain was clear and active, im-patient to accept the incongruity of her situation.

Could this really be the home of a wealthy man, eccentric or otherwise? The fire had died in the night, and the room was cold and chilly, significant of the lack of any adequate heating system. The square of carpet that protected her feet from the icy contact of the lino was made of the cheapest materials, and even the curtains hanging at the windows had seen better days.

The curtains aroused her to the fact that the previous even-ing, darkness had prevented her from seeing anything beyond the windows. Now she slipped out of bed and ran across the room, drawing back the curtains and peering out.

The view was breathtaking, making her forget the cold. The

early morning sunlight was gilding the breakers which rolled continuously into the shoreline, shadowing the curve of headland which stretched into the distance, ruggedly formidable. Beneath her windows, a brief grassy sward gave on to the cliff edge, and the rocks which shattered the waves into flurries of spume were hidden below their vertical face.

The sense of excitement she had felt so briefly the night before returned again. No matter what happened, she was not sorry she had come here. She was not foolish enough to deceive herself that it was going to be easy. There were undercurrents here which she had never even suspected at the time of her acceptance of the position, but no matter how brief her visit, she would not have missed the experience. And what kind of an experience might it be, living in the house of an ex-mercenary, who, according to Mr. Hollister, had hated his own brother, and whose brother's wife obviously regarded him as her personal property. Was that why the brothers had quarrelled? Had they both loved Nerys? And now that his brother was dead, was he simply waiting until a decent interval had elapsed before making her his wife? Curiously enough, she found something distasteful about that idea. But why? Unless, as her instincts told her, it was because William's position might well be made intolerable by such an event.

With a shrug, she turned and surveyed the room behind her. Although it was uninspiring at the moment, with newly painted woodwork, some decent wall covering, a warmly fitted carpet, and fresh curtains and covers, it would look rather splendid. Its proportions were generous, and the ceiling mouldings were cleverly elaborate, if a little grubby right now. The fireplace had a real marble mantel, and the tarnished fittings in the grate could easily be cleaned.

So why hadn't it been done—along with the central heating system she had longed for the previous evening? The bathroom adjoining the bedroom had been an ice-box the night before, and while the water had been reasonably hot from the taps, its coppery tinge had indicated the age of the boiler. If Rhys Llewellyn—no, *Edwards*—was a wealthy man, why didn't he use some of his money to put his house in order?

Realising she was getting frozen just standing there in her nightgown, she walked briskly across the room to the bathroom door. A noisy gurgling in the pipes indicated that someone else was getting up, too, and she consulted her watch for the first time that morning. It was a little after seven-thirty, and she hurried over her teeth-cleaning, forgoing the bath she had promised herself in her efforts to be ready for breakfast at eight.

She dressed in a three-quarter-length skirt of navy blue wool, teaming it with a white blouse and navy tank top. She was confident she looked neat and businesslike, and regarded her hair with some misgivings before deciding to secure it with a leather slide at her nape. She was applying a faint eyeliner when there was a knock at her door, and frowning slightly, she went to open it.

To her surprise, William stood outside, wrapped in the same grey dressing gown he had been wearing the night before, although now his hair was rumpled from the pillow. His face looked less feverish this morning, and she stepped back almost automatically, allowing him to enter the room.

"I'm not disturbing you, am I?" he asked, closing the door behind him, as though the question was purely rhetorical. "But I didn't have a chance to speak to you last night, and I wanted to welcome you to Devil's Mount."

Julie was touched. "Well—thank you, William. But for you, I wouldn't be here."

"I know." He grinned conspiratorially, and she wondered what that grin was supposed to mean. "But you are here, aren't you, and I, for one, am—delighted!"

Julie finished stroking the brush across her lashes, and putting it away, gave him a wry look. "I'm glad someone is."

"Oh, you mean Nerys?" He misunderstood her remark. "Yes, she wasn't very pleased, was she? But I suppose that's only natural. She doesn't like competition—not from anyone."

Julie gasped. "I'm not competition!" she exclaimed. Then: "In any case, that's not what I meant."

"They had one hell of a row last night, my father and Nerys," William went on with evident relish, and although Julie was curious to know why, she knew she had to stop him from gossiping to her.

"Your father's affairs are no concern of mine," she put in hastily. "It was nice of you to come here, William, and I expect we'll be seeing a lot of one another from now on, but right at this moment I have to go down to breakfast. It's after eight o'clock."

"I shouldn't worry about that," remarked William, making no attempt to leave, but instead fingering the bottles on the stand in front of her, opening jars of cold cream and skin perfume, inhaling their fragrance with apparent enjoyment. "My father may demand punctuality in others, but he rarely practises it himself."

"Is that so?" Julie took a flagon of perfumed spray out of his enquiring fingers, and set it back on the marble-surfaced washstand. "Nevertheless, I think on my first day I ought to make an effort, don't you?"

"He was late meeting you at the station yesterday evening, wasn't he?"

Julie's mouth turned down at the corners. "I understand that was hardly his fault."

William looked petulant. "I know. I made a scene. I guessed he'd have to tell you!"

"I was angry with him. I'd been waiting almost half an hour!" exclaimed Julie indignantly.

William's expression cleared. "*You*—were angry with

him!" He chuckled delightedly. "What did he say?"

Julie checked her appearance in the mirror. "I don't think that's any concern of yours!" she stated firmly, picking up her bag. "Now—you'll have to excuse me."

William looked disappointed. "Can't you stay and talk just a little while longer? No one ever talks to me."

Julie sighed. "What about your cousin?"

"Dulcie?" William was aghast. "You can't be serious. What?—talk to that tale-bearing little bitch—"

"*William!*" Julie was shocked. "Don't speak about your cousin in that way."

"Why not?" William was unrepentant. "She is. Exactly like her mother."

"That will do, William." Julie could not allow him to go on. He had already said too much. Taking the initiative, she swung open the door again on the draughty corridor beyond. "After you."

William hunched his thin shoulders, and walked ahead of her out of the room. Unwillingly, her sympathies were aroused by his air of wounded vulnerability, and although she had half expected him to march off in a huff, she was relieved when he halted just outside the door and faced her again.

"Will you come and see me at lunchtime?" he asked, his features hopefully appealing, and Julie did not know how to refuse him. "My room is further along here." He pointed along the corridor which was an extension of the gallery above the hall. "The third door—see? I'm not allowed to get up until after lunch."

Julie shook her head. "Then what are you doing here?"

"I told you—I wanted to see you. Well? Will you come?"

Julie bit her lip. "I suppose so. Now, hurry back to your room. Don't go catching any more cold. I want you to show me around, and you can't do that if you persist in putting up your temperature."

William's face brightened considerably. "If the weather stays fine, I should be able to go outside within the week," he told her.

"That's good. Now, I must go."

"Do you know where?"

"Where what?"

"Where to go? To have breakfast?"

Julie hesitated. "Why, no, I don't think I do."

William nodded. "I thought not. Well, the door to the dining room is to your right at the foot of the stairs. But don't be surprised if you eat alone. Nerys never rises much before eleven and my father, as I've said, doesn't always practise what he preaches."

Julie ignored this, and thanking him for the information, set off along the corridor towards the gallery above the hall. Although it wasn't quite as cold now as it had been the night before, the lack of heating about the place quickened her step, and she ignored the general air of neglect about the house. The hall was deserted, but following William's directions, she opened the door to her right and found herself in a large room, overlooking the cliffs as her room did above. To boast its right to being called a dining room, there was a long table, presently covered by a rather grey-looking white cloth, and an equally long sideboard, with carved fittings and tarnished brass handles, which should have supported serving dishes. But the white cloth was the only sign of the room's designation, and the twelve ladder-backed chairs which flanked the sides and both ends of the table were a mocking salute to times past.

Julie walked uncertainly into the room, wondering whether there was a bell she should ring, or whether indeed she should take the matter into her own hands and go looking for the kitchen. This enormous room was not meant to be used by one person alone, and besides, it, too, was exceedingly chilly, in spite of the fire crackling in a wide grate.

She looked round when the door behind her opened, but was disappointed to find only Dulcie's sulky little face staring at her. The child hovered indecisively in the doorway, allowing draughts of icy air from the hall to penetrate the room, and Julie sighed rather impatiently.

"Are you coming in?" she enquired, in what she hoped was a friendly tone, but Dulcie just continued to stare.

"Are you going to have breakfast with me?" Julie tried another overture, but Dulcie merely screwed up her face into an ugly grimace, allowed the length of her tongue to appear between the twisted contours of her lips, and then disappeared out of the door again before her startled victim could make any protest.

Well! Julie went to stand with her back to the fire, feeling distinctly put out. So that was Uncle Rhys' "favourite", was it? Julie was inclined to favour William's estimate just at that moment. What a rude little girl! Her hands itched to take the child and put her over her knee and administer several hard slaps to her small rear.

When the door opened a second time, she turned sharply, prepared to tell Dulcie, in no uncertain terms, exactly what she thought of her behaviour. But instead of the child, Rhys Llewellyn—or should she call him Rhys Edwards now?— entered the room. His eyes flickered over Julie's unknowingly aggressive stance, and then he said sardonically:

"Now let me guess what you're going to say . . . your room is cold, your bed wasn't comfortable . . . or you had no idea what a remote place this was going to be when you accepted the post?"

Julie endeavoured not to be intimidated by his remarks. "I was going to say none of those things, actually," she replied.

"No?"

"No."

"Then am I to be privileged to know what words trembled

on your tongue as I came through that door?"

"If it pleases you." Julie tried to sound indifferent. "My words were to have been—*what an ignorant, ill-mannered little girl you are!*"

"Ah!" Comprehension deepened the lines beside his mouth. "I gather my niece has already presented herself."

"You could say that."

Rhys flexed his back muscles, and walked further into the room with that curiously stiff gait she had noticed before. "You must forgive Dulcie. She's a lonely child, too much in the company of adults, and I'm afraid a little spoilt in consequence."

"A little?" echoed Julie meaningly, and his dark eyes narrowed.

"She is only six, Miss Wood," he countered drily. "No great age, you must agree."

"Old enough to know the difference between being naughty —and downright rude!" retorted Julie.

Rhys shrugged, the movement parting the lapels of the black leather waistcoat he was wearing over a bronze denim shirt. "Would you have me discipline the child, Miss Wood? Don't you think there's enough violence in the world without creating more for ourselves?"

Julie flushed. "It's nothing to do with me what you decide to do."

"No, it's not," he agreed briefly, and she was still smarting under that, in her eyes, unwarranted reproof, when the door opened again to admit a middle-aged woman in a gingham overall, carrying a heavy silver tray.

Rhys moved to take the tray from the woman, but she indicated that she could manage and set it down with evident relief on the end of the table. Now Julie could see that the tray held covered dishes and cereal bowls, toast and coffee cups, and a tall percolator.

62

"It smells good, Mrs. Evans," remarked her employer, approaching the table as the woman went to get silver cutlery from a drawer in the sideboard. "Oh, and I don't believe you've met my new secretary, have you? Miss Wood, this is Mrs. Evans, she's our cook and housekeeper rolled into one."

Julie said "Good morning" in return to the housekeeper's mumbled greeting, but she had the distinct feeling that Mrs. Evans did not want her here any more than did Nerys Edwards. She wondered why. Perhaps the housekeeper was a particular crony of Rhys Edwards' sister-in-law, and took her orders from her. And then another thought struck her. No doubt, this had been Nerys's home, as the wife of the first Marquis of Llantreath, for a great number of years. Yet remembering the neglected state of the hall, and this room's shortcomings, Julie decided that Mrs. Evans' qualifications as a housekeeper were sadly lacking.

Still, the food did smell delicious, and Julie found she was ravenously hungry, surprisingly so after the hostility of the last few minutes. Mrs. Evans departed after setting two places at the end of the long table, and plugging the percolator into a connection beside the sideboard. Rhys Edwards waited until the door had closed behind her, then he indicated that Julie should sit down.

"Now, what will you have?" he asked, after she was settled, and he had come to take the chair at the end of the table. "Fruit juice? I see Mrs. Evans has forgotten to bring any, but I'm sure we have orange juice in the refrigerator."

"I'll have some cornflakes," replied Julie stiffly, choosing something that was available, and he handed her a bowl and one of the individual packets standing on the tray.

While she poured out the cornflakes and added milk and sugar, Rhys examined the plates beneath their metal covers. An aroma of bacon and sausages came to Julie's nostrils, and she looked up to find him watching her and not eating himself.

Consequently, colour filled her cheeks again, and he made a deprecating gesture.

"I'm sorry," he said, a half smile tugging at the corners of his thin mouth, "but I'm not accustomed to seeing anyone enjoy their food as you do. William eats sparingly, and Dulcie . . . Well, she eats too many of the wrong things between meals to really do justice to her appetite."

If his apology was intended to put Julie at her ease, it succeeded in doing quite the opposite. She felt ridiculously like a schoolgirl, wolfing a midnight feast, and the fact that the sun was shining outside the tall windows made little difference to her embarrassment. There was nothing she could say that would not sound trite, but after that she kept an eye on him, waiting until he started eating himself before continuing with her meal. She noticed he ate very little considering he was such a big man, but did not have the nerve to comment upon it.

When she was drinking her second cup of coffee, he asked her whether she would mind if he lit a cigar. Shaking her head, Julie watched as he lighted a spill from the fire, applying it to the end of the narrow cigar with a steady hand. Then he turned to face her, and she waited for him to speak.

"Are you disappointed?" he asked, disconcerting her.

"Disappointed?" She frowned.

"With Devil's Mount? You must have had some notion of the kind of place it would be."

"Oh, I see." Julie recovered her composure. "Well, I haven't really given it a lot of thought. It's—very big."

"And very draughty, and very old," he added dryly. "I am aware of its shortcomings. But I like it. I was born here, and I lived here until I was old enough to be sent away to school. After that—well, after that, it was different."

Julie listened with interest. "And—your name is—Edwards?"

His features hardened. "I gather the name means something

64

to you. Thomas thought it might."

"Thomas?" Julie was momentarily confused.

"Henry Thomas. My solicitor. You read the columns of the gutter press, I assume."

Julie gasped. "I don't know what you mean!"

"But you do know my name."

"You told me it was Llewellyn—"

"I beg your pardon, you assumed that."

"Well, it was the name William used."

"Agreed."

"But your name is—Edwards?"

"Llewellyn-Edwards, to be exact. Llewellyn was my mother's name." He sighed, studying the glowing tip of his cigar. "So what do you know of me, Miss Wood? What juicy pieces of gossip have you heard?"

Julie wished she had not started this. "I—I just wanted to know what I'm supposed to call you," she said, with remarkable calmness.

His eyes narrowed, their darkness glittering between the thick lashes. "You're not about to offer your resignation, then?"

"Why should I?" Julie felt a twinge of anxiety in spite of her brave statement. "I—couldn't help noticing how your—sister-in-law introduced herself last evening, and—and Haggar called you Mr. *Edwards*."

He was watching her closely, and she wondered whether he entirely believed her. His smile when it appeared was vaguely sardonic, but he shrugged and said: "Very well, Miss Wood, shall we get to work?"

Julie licked her lips. "And—I'm to call you Mr. Edwards?"

A mocking quirk lifted one dark eyebrow. "You may call me Rhys, if you prefer it," he replied wryly, and her colour deepened once more.

"Thank you, Mr. Edwards."

He shook his head as he walked towards the door, and following him, Julie wondered at her own determination to stay here and make a success of this job. It was so different from what she had expected, and after what Mr. Hollister had told her, she ought to be wary of this man. But in spite of her antagonism towards him, their relationship was stimulating, in a way she had hitherto never experienced before.

They crossed the chilly hall and Rhys opened the door into a comparatively small room by Devil's Mount standards, but which was still generous when compared to her mother's sitting room back home. It was obviously the library, the walls lined from floor to ceiling with books, and a narrow gallery reached by an iron ladder gave access to those nearest the top. There was a musty odour of ancient leather and mouldering decay, and not even another of the fires, which seemed necessary everywhere, had been able to dispel the damp atmosphere. Julie couldn't suppress a shiver, and Rhys regarded her frowningly.

"You're cold?"

"Only a little." Julie looked round the room with interest. "I've never seen a library like this outside of a stately home."

"And Devil's Mount is no stately home," he commented dryly. "I know. But I intend it to be. Or at least, a—home."

Julie advanced into the room across the beige patterned carpet, halting beside a leather-tooled desk on which reposed a tray of papers and a modern typewriter, which looked slightly incongruous in these surroundings. There was a buttoned leather armchair, soft and squashy, and totally unsuitable for her to work from, a couple of upright dining chairs, and a Victorian chaise-longue beside the fireplace. She looked expectantly towards her employer and he moved from his position by the door to indicate that she should sit down at the desk.

"I prefer to walk about while I'm dictating," he said, one hand moving to support a momentary stretching of his spine.

66

"Please—sit down. We must discuss the methods I want to employ."

Julie looked doubtfully at the soft buttoned leather. "I'd rather use one of those," she said, pointing towards the dining chairs. "This is—too low."

"All right." He pushed the leather armchair aside, and set a tapestry-seated chair in its place. "Remind me to acquire an office chair next time I go into Llantreath."

"That's not necessary—" she began awkwardly, but he gave her a wry look.

"I can afford it," he told her, and she was silent.

After she was seated, he came to the desk and pulled open several drawers at the right-hand side. His nearness was disturbing, she found, particularly as she could smell the soap he used and the warm heat of his body.

"Paper," he said, and she tried to concentrate on what he was showing her. "Carbons. Typewriter ribbons. I think that's everything you need. Oh, and these pads and pencils, of course."

"Yes." It was inadequate, but it was all she could manage right at that moment, and he nodded.

"You needn't bother trying to open the drawers at the other side," he went on. "They're locked, and their contents need not concern you."

Julie was stung to impulsive defence. "I was not about to pry, Mr. Edwards."

"I'm sure you weren't." He straightened to look down into her indignant face, and she averted her eyes from his compelling gaze. "Now—so far as working methods are concerned, I suggest I dictate in the morning, you transcribe what I've dictated in the afternoon, and then I can read the typescript in the evening and decide whether any alterations need to be made." He paused, and when she said nothing, added: "Does that sound reasonable to you?"

Julie nodded.

"Is there anything you want to ask, Miss Wood?"

"No." She glanced up at him then. "What could there be?"

"Indeed." He moved away towards the marble fireplace, throwing the stub of his cigar into the flames. "What indeed?"

Julie sighed. "There is one thing . . ."

"Yes." He turned to face her, his hands thrust deep into the pockets of moccasin-leather pants.

"It's—William, actually. Would you mind if I had my lunch with him?"

He frowned then. "You've—spoken to William this morning?"

Julie felt uncomfortable under that accusing stare. "Yes. Oh, yes. But, please, don't be angry with him. He came to my room. He wanted to welcome me to Devil's Mount, and—and you stopped him last night."

Rhys's expression was not encouraging. "In spite of what you may have heard to the contrary, Miss Wood, you are not here to be a companion to my son."

"I never thought I was—"

"I suggest you think twice before committing yourself to a situation that could very easily get out of hand."

"What do you mean?"

"You've seen William. You know what he's like—what he's capable of. Aren't you afraid he may demand more of your time than you will ultimately be prepared to give?"

Julie moved her shoulders in a defensive gesture. "He's lonely, that's all," she said. Then, looking at him squarely: "How much time do you give to your son, Mr. Edwards?"

As soon as the words were uttered, she wished she could withdraw them. Did she went to be dismissed from this post before she had even begun? What business was it of hers how the members of this family conducted their affairs?

His eyes could have challenged agate for hardness, and she found it increasingly difficult to sustain their penetration. He seemed to be staring into her very soul, stripping away her shallow defences, making her aware of her own hopeless inadequacy. Who was she to dare to criticize him, to take him to task for his own shortcomings when she really knew so little of his background—his wants, his needs, his loyalties? But someone had to stand up for William, she justified herself silently, aware that just now she would have traded that right for a minute's space to breathe without constriction.

However, when he spoke, his tone was quiet, if no less compelling. "I see my son has found himself a champion at last," he said, withdrawing his hands from his pockets and flexing them by his sides. "What possible power has he exerted over you that you should feel such protection for him? Believe me, William is no shorn lamb."

Julie shook her head. "When—when children are difficult—"

"You're little more than a child yourself, Miss Wood!"

"—there's usually a reason behind it. I don't think William is a very—happy child," she finished rather breathlessly.

"Don't you?" There was impatience in his tone.

"No." She had to go on now she had started. "You say he's been thrown out of three schools. Haven't you ever asked yourself why?"

"Spare me the psychoanalysis, Miss Wood!" he retorted shortly. "Right now, *you* are beginning to sound like more trouble than William has ever done."

Julie was dismayed. "You—you asked me if there was anything I wanted to say," she exclaimed indignantly.

"No. *I* said—was there anything you wanted to ask," he corrected her harshly. "As I keep having to remind you, Miss Wood, you are not here for William's benefit, nor particularly for mine! However, if you prefer governessing to being my secretary, then I suggest you answer different advertisements in future!"

Julie felt foolish. "I'm sorry," she muttered with ill grace.

"No, you're not. You're just paying lip service." He approached the desk and for a moment she wondered what he was going to do and tensed because of it. But he merely lifted the metal tray containing the loose papers and said quietly: "I suggest we deal with a few of these first."

Julie reached for her pad and pencil. It was obvious that so far as he was concerned their conversation was at an end. She chewed irritably on the end of her pencil. So much for her intervention on William's behalf. If anything, she had made the situation even more fraught than it had been before. And he still hadn't given her permission to have lunch with his son.

CHAPTER FIVE

JULIE let herself into her bedroom and closed the door, leaning back against it rather weakly. Her first morning's work was over, and although her fingers ached from keeping up with the flow of his dictation, it was her mind, her sensitivities, which felt most abused by his bruising narrative.

Of course, she had had no experience of working with a writer before, and consequently, her ideas of someone composing a novel inclined towards the romantic image imposed by films of poets and artists of another era. The reality was much different. Rhys Edwards did not need to wait for inspiration, he did not need to search for words to express himself. He knew exactly what he wanted to say, and how he wanted to say it, and the three thousand words or so he had dictated that morning had already built up a picture that tortured Julie's fertile imagination.

Until now, she had not given a lot of thought to the kind of book her employer might be intending to write. Besides, as he had apparently not written a novel before, it had not seemed unreasonable to suppose that perhaps what he wrote would not be acceptable. But even without the publishers' letter confirming their interest in the project, Julie knew that the story Rhys Edwards was telling was sure-fire material. It was a piece of compelling fiction which no one could be quite sure was not factual, with just sufficient information, just sufficient use of known names, to make the plot ambiguous.

As yet, they had barely touched on the main theme of the story, but his descriptions of the prison conditions in a guerilla stronghold in Central Africa were horrifying. The man who, Rhys had explained, was to be the main character in the book was being held by the guerillas, and his treatment at their hands aroused all Julie's sympathies and indignation. There was a wealth of feeling in the words Rhys used, and taking it all down on her notepad, Julie felt herself to be an actual part of the creation. In consequence now, she felt drained, both physically and spiritually, aware that she had never experienced anything so mentally exhausting in her life.

Straightening away from the door, she walked across the room, catching a glimpse of herself in the long wardrobe mirrors. There was a pencil smudge on her chin and her hair was escaping in untidy strands across the dark wool of her tank top. But it was her eyes which drew her attention, dark and disturbed, the lids heavy with weariness. A faint flush of colour crept up under her skin. She looked different, aware. Almost as though she had just indulged in some devastating emotional scene. Her tongue appeared as she wet lips suddenly dry with dismay. Was this how Rhys Edwards had seen her? Was he aware that he had, in some strange way, seduced her with his words?

As soon as the thought entered her head, she dismissed it. Heavens, she was becoming fanciful! She was allowing his undoubted literary ability to assume qualities it simply did not possess. She had worked hard all morning, she was tired. What more natural than that her eyes should mirror that purely physical state?

Without asking herself why, she marched into the bathroom, and sluiced her face thoroughly under the tap. Fortunately, there seemed no shortage of hot water, although she used it barely lukewarm in an effort to cool her heated cheeks. She was brushing her hair when someone knocked at her door.

Taking a deep breath, she went to answer it, half expecting to find William outside as before, but instead it was Mrs. Evans. The housekeeper did not appear any too pleased at being obliged to deliver messages, and she said shortly:

72

"Mr. Edwards said to tell you your lunch is being served in Master William's room."

Julie was surprised and relieved. At least that would enable her to avoid another confrontation with her employer until she was sure she was quite in control of herself.

"Thank you for letting me know," she acknowledged with a smile, but the housekeeper turned away.

"Better hurry up before it gets cold," she muttered, as she went away along the corridor, and Julie hastily secured her hair and made her way to William's room.

It was not difficult to find. His door was ajar, and when he heard her footsteps, he called: "In here. Julie, I'm here!"

Julie pushed open the door into a room not unlike her own. There was the same high ceiling, the same shabby appointments, the same marble fireplace. Only the bed was different. William's bed was a simple divan, and he was sitting up in it, looking towards the door, a grin of satisfaction spreading over his thin features. Beside him, a trolley had been unfolded to form a small circular table set with plates and serving dishes.

"Come on in," called William, when she hesitated in the doorway. "I didn't feel hungry at first, but when Mrs. Evans told me you were joining me, Julie, I knew I was going to enjoy my lunch."

Julie sighed, closing the door so that the heat generated by the fire should not all escape. "I don't remember giving you permission to call me Julie," she observed, approaching the bed.

"Well, I can't call you Miss Wood all the time," he protested, looking appealingly up at her. "I mean—well, you are only four years older than me, you know."

"Four years is quite a considerable time at your age," she retorted, and he made a face.

"Now you sound just like my father," he grumbled. "Oh, sit

73

down. You can use that chair." He indicated a basket-woven bedroom chair. "You must be hungry after working all morning."

"Yes." Julie brought the chair to the trolley-table and sat down. "It has been rather hectic."

"I know." William grinned maliciously. "Dulcie's had her nose put right out of joint."

"What do you mean?" Julie frowned.

"Well, she did come to the library, didn't she? I mean, she came up here grumbling about my father turning her away."

"Oh, I see. Yes." Julie remembered that moment when the door had opened and Dulcie's small face had appeared. But this time Rhys had had no time for her, sending her away with evident impatience, intent on the work he was doing to the exclusion of all else.

"She said she doesn't like you," went on William, clearly determined to arouse Julie's annoyance and succeeding, except that she was equally determined that he should not know about it.

"Dulcie is only six years old," she said, using the defence Rhys had used earlier in the day. "I imagine living here, in such remote surroundings, she's not really used to mixing with other people."

William snorted. "She hasn't lived here long enough to be affected by it, one way or the other!"

Julie had been taking the lids off the serving dishes, discovering a delicious-smelling meat and vegetable stew, to be followed by apple pie and custard. But she looked up at his words, curious in spite of herself. "What do you mean?" she asked. "Wasn't this—I mean, isn't this—" She floundered, aware that she had almost committed herself to more knowledge than she was known to possess. "Isn't this—Dulcie's home?" she finished lamely.

"I suppose it is now," agreed William dourly, helping him-

74

self to the stew and then handing the ladle to Julie. "But she doesn't like it any more than her mother does."

Julie ladled some of the stew on to her own plate, and picking up her fork began to eat. It was not her affair, she was telling herself impatiently, aware that William's words offered a tantalising challenge. It was no good allowing herself to become involved with the personal affairs of the occupants of Devil's Mount. She was here to do a job of work and goodness knows, that was going to be difficult enough, without making herself a party to William's petty intrigues. All the same, curiosity was a trying companion.

Making an effort to divert their conversation into less personal channels, she said: "This stew is delicious, isn't it? Just what we need on a cold day like today."

William allowed that it was all right. "Mrs. Evans isn't a bad cook," he conceded grudgingly, "but she's not much good at anything else. She can't keep staff, you know. But perhaps that's because people round here don't like her. She comes from up north, you see."

"Up north?" Julie looked at him disbelievingly. "She has a distinct Welsh accent."

"I know. But she's from Bangor. That's 'up north' to these people."

He spoke scathingly, and Julie said: "Don't be so patronising, William!" in reproving tones.

"Well, it's true." He was not to be outdone. "We have had girls working here, girls from the village. But they don't really like us either, I suppose, so perhaps it's not all Mrs. Evans' fault."

"I think you're exaggerating, William," she retorted, with some asperity, finishing the stew on her plate and pushing it aside. "You seem to have a hang-up about people not liking you. Perhaps you don't try hard enough to like them."

"My father says that sometimes people get their priorities

75

mixed up. He doesn't seem to care if people don't like him. But I do."

Julie sighed, irritation making her reckless. "Why should you assume that the people from the village don't like you?"

"Because of Uncle Richard."

Julie picked up a knife. It seemed impossible not to return to the problems of this family. "Would you like a piece of apple pie?" she asked, cutting into the crisp pastry, and William sighed rather exaggeratedly.

"Do you want to know about Uncle Richard?" he asked, after she had set a dish of fruit pie and custard in front of him.

Julie tackled her own dessert. "Not particularly, William. I think I'd rather hear about you. How long is it since you—left school?"

"My last school, you mean?" William considered the question. "Oh—about five months, I suppose."

"Five months!"

"Well, there was the summer holidays, you see, so I suppose actually it has only been about two months."

Julie shook her head. "And are you going back?"

"I can't. They won't let me. My father was asked to take me away at the end of last term."

The question "Why?" hovered on Julie's lips, but again she kept silent. William's problems were just as personal to the family as anyone's. But this time William did not ask whether she was interested. He plunged straight on with his explanation.

"You see, when Uncle Richard was killed, I knew Da would come home. Nerys would make sure of that. And he'd always said he'd open up Devil's Mount again, and I couldn't risk her persuading him to stay in London, when I wanted so much to live here—"

Julie interrupted him then. "William, please! This has nothing to do with me. You will persist in discussing your family's

76

private affairs. I was only curious to know how much of a gap in your education there had been.''

William hunched his thin shoulders, the bones sticking through the cotton material of his striped pyjamas. Whether it was deliberate or not, Julie could not be sure, but he could assume a pathetic air which aroused all her sympathies.

"I thought you'd be someone I could talk to," he muttered, sniffing resentfully. "I thought you'd be interested. But I suppose you only came here out of curiosity."

"That's not true!" Julie stared at him impatiently. "You know very well how I came to be here."

"But you didn't have to accept the job, did you? I mean, after you found out I'd been lying, you could have turned it down. What changed your mind? Meeting my father? Women like my father. That was why he wanted someone older for the job. So that Nerys wouldn't object!"

"William!" Julie pushed her dish aside and began gathering the dirty plates together. "Whatever your father's reasons for employing me, and you must know that you were instrumental in achieving that, I'm here now and I'm not—regretting it."

"You're not?" William looked up at her.

"No. But I shall be if you persist in using me as a sounding board for your biased speculations. I'm not interested in the whys and wherefores, only in the present. I want us to be friends, too. But not so we can gossip about every other member of the household!"

William regarded her broodingly. "What else is there to talk about?"

Julie sighed. "Why, heaps of things. As soon as you're up and about again, we'll go for walks, explore the cliffs, go into the village . . ." She paused. "What are you interested in, yourself? Do you like reading—or music? Do you play an instrument?"

"Do you?"

77

Julie shook her head. "We were talking about you. But yes, as a matter of fact, I play the guitar. Not very well, but well enough to amuse myself."

"Have you brought it with you?"

Julie chuckled. "You must be joking! What would your father have said if I'd arrived at Devil's Mount complete with guitar case? I'm here to be a secretary, not an entertainer."

William smiled then, and his lean features fleetingly mirrored a little of his father's charm. She felt an overwhelming sense of compassion towards him, realising that since coming here William's world had been limited to the kind of introspection that bred his fantasies about people not liking him. Somehow, at weekends maybe, she would have to find time for William, and she realised with a pang that free time was going to be a very sparse commodity at Devil's Mount.

When she returned to the library after lunching with William to transcribe the pages of shorthand she had taken down that morning, there was no sign of her employer. Not that she needed his assistance. He had explained his working methods very clearly that morning, and no doubt he had other duties to attend to during the afternoon. However, he had not said how many copies he wanted of the typescript, and she hesitated for a while before inserting two carbons. She had completed more than half the copy when Nerys appeared.

This afternoon, the older girl was dressed in a soft cashmere sweater and a finely pleated skirt, both in shades of lilac which toned with her lipstick and eyeshadow. The fluffy curls which framed her small face gave her a childlike air, but there was nothing innocent about the long, purple-coated nails which plucked at the double string of pearls about her slender throat. She came into the room without invitation, and looked casually over Julie's shoulder at the page in the typewriter.

"Working hard, Miss Wood?" she queried silkily.

Julie felt like covering the page with her hands. She didn't know whether Rhys Edwards would approve of anyone else reading his novel until it was finished. With a flick of her wrist, she unwound the page, screwing it up into a ball and dropping it into the waste bin. Then, as she took three clean pages and inserted carbons between them, she managed to cover the pages she had already typed with a blank sheet.

"That was careless," she said, with feigned annoyance. "It's so important to be—accurate."

Nerys had straightened when Julie pulled out the sheets from the machine, and her expression revealed she was not deceived by the younger girl's behaviour.

"So efficient," she murmured, leaving the desk to cross to the windows. "I must congratulate Rhys on his choice of typist."

The use of the word "typist" was deliberate, but Julie didn't mind. Until she knew the situation here better, she was prepared to suffer a little insolence.

"Thank you," she said now, as though accepting Nerys's sarcasm as a compliment, and was gratified to see those lilac-painted lips tighten with annoyance.

"Tell me, Miss Wood," Nerys hadn't finished with her yet, "whatever attracted a girl like yourself to work in a place like this?" She spread a hand expressively.

Julie hesitated. "It's—different," she said at last. "I felt like a change of scene."

"But you used to live in London, I understand."

"Just outside, actually."

"But you worked in London."

"Yes."

"And you'd exchange that, for *this*!"

"I don't know what you mean, Mrs. Edwards."

"Perhaps you are not aware that my husband was the Marquis of Llantreath, Miss Wood. Although I must admit that now my husband is dead Rhys does not intend to use the title, I still consider myself *Lady* Llantreath, do you understand?"

Julie pressed her lips together for a moment. Then she nodded. "Yes, my lady," she said obediently.

Nerys half smiled. "So you don't think there's any difference in working here from working in London?"

"I didn't say that exactly. It's just that—well, my work in London was boring. I worked in a solicitor's office, and it was very repetitious. Working for—Mr. Edwards is—interesting."

"I see." Nerys folded her arms, her fingers beating a silent tattoo against her sleeve. "And William? I believe you've become very friendly with him."

"I like him, yes."

"When all around you did not," misquoted Nerys dryly. "You realise he is a problem child? That he can summon these asthmatic attacks to suit himself?"

Here we go again, thought Julie, with resignation. But she could not allow Nerys to get away with that.

"I think any child who suffers from something as physically frightening as asthma deserves some sympathy, Mrs.—I mean, my lady."

"But William gets sympathy," snapped Nerys impatiently. "Too much sympathy, in my opinion. He's always been the same. He can't bear to be ignored, so he simulates these attacks to attract attention to himself."

Julie looked down at the typewriter. "I expect he misses having a mother," she volunteered quietly.

"*A mother!*" Nerys was scathing. "William's mother never cared a hang for him! She abandoned him on the steps of a children's home when he was barely five days old! That's how much she cared for him."

Julie's eyes were troubled as she listened to what Nerys was saying. How could any woman do that to her child? Without even taking the trouble to ensure that he had been taken in?

And why hadn't his father stopped her? How did William come to be living with Rhys now?.

So many questions, and she could not ask them. She saw Nerys watching her, and realised she was probably having a struggle, too. The desire to confide was irresistible, but satisfying Julie's curiosity was not.

"Where is your employer?" Nerys asked now, and Julie shook her head.

"I haven't seen him since before lunch."

"No." Nerys nodded, moving slowly towards the door again. "I expect he's gone to get some stores for Mrs. Evans." She broke off. "I'll leave you to your labours, Miss Wood. Don't worry about joining us for dinner this evening. I expect after working all day, you'll be glad of some time on your own."

The door closed behind her before Julie could make any denial, but she wondered afterwards whether that was not a good thing. Did she want to join the members of the family for dinner, or would it not indeed be simpler to have her meal served in her room? She did deserve some free time, as Nerys had said, although her reasons for saying it might have undercurrents Julie did not want to consider. There were things that bore consideration, though. William had been right about his aunt's interest in her brother-in-law. And if Nerys was used to living in London, as it appeared, Rhys must hold some strong attraction for her to bring her to the wilds of Wales in winter, to this house with its evident lack of amenities and decaying splendour.

It was still daylight, albeit the sun was rapidly losing its brilliance, when Julie finished the typescript, and on impulse, she collected her coat and waterproof boots from her room, and let herself out the front door.

The wind which had whistled gently round the house all day was rising, and she was glad of the long scarf she had wound round her neck. Her hair soon loosened itself from any confining influence, and blew about her face as she descended the stone steps and reached the gravelled sweep of the drive. Following the sound of the sea, she walked round the house, exhilarated by the buffeting of the wind and the clear sharp scent of the ocean.

She came, as she had expected she would, to the sweep of turf that inclined towards the cliffs, and thrusting her hands into the deep pockets of her tweed coat, she stood there watching the incoming breakers rolling shorewards.

But it was not enough. The actual shoreline was hidden below the cliffs, and rather recklessly she approached the edge. The wind was much stronger here, and rather than risk being blown over, she got down on to her knees and peered down the cliff face.

A sharp incline gave on to a mossy shelf, and from the shelf she could see a rugged pathway leading down to the rocks below. Dangerous enough, in these conditions, but accessible on calm days. She and William could climb down there easily.

With the sun turning the sea to molten fire, the sky a blending of orange through green to palest blue, the bend of the headland casting a darkening shadow over the cruel teeth of the rocks, it was a majestic sight, and she wondered at her own feeling of satisfaction in it. That she, a town girl born and bred, restless with the life she had been leading there, and in search of new excitement, should find so much fulfilment in the reality of being here, on this remote coastline, was rather startling. But it was more than this view, or the house, or even the grip of the work she was doing; it was the people in the house who provided the greatest challenge, and while she told herself it was her sympathy for William which made her so aware of his father, she acknowledged, in a moment of absolute truthfulness, that it was more than that. And that was the excitement she had found . . .

CHAPTER SIX

In fact, Julie did have dinner with the family that evening, at the long table in the dining room, serving themselves from the sideboard which looked only slightly less dusty than it had done that morning. But it was through no choice of her own. On the contrary, after those moments of self-enlightenment on the cliffs, she would have welcomed the solitude of her room, welcomed the time to collect and assimilate her thoughts before becoming involved with her employer again. But William had other ideas.

He was waiting for her when she came back from her walk. Perhaps he had seen her from his windows as he dressed. But now he was downstairs, and the colour in his usually pale cheeks bore witness to the fact that he was still far from well. He insisted that they had tea together, in the living room, where she had glimpsed him briefly the night before, and although she guessed this was something else of which Nerys would not approve, she hadn't the heart to refuse him.

The living room was quite a comfortable room, with inevitably shabby leather chairs, and an enormous chesterfield, upholstered in dark brown velvet, that was wearing thin in places. The square of carpet still maintained a certain softness underfoot, matching the long beige and brown patterned curtains that framed windows overlooking the cliffs on the opposite side of the house from those she had been exploring. After the coldness of the wind outside, the logs burning in the grate were very welcoming, and after removing her coat, Julie held her hands out to the blaze.

Then she noticed the tea trolley set to one side of the couch, but before she could say anything, William exclaimed: "You must be dying for a cup of tea after freezing out there."

"You were very sure I'd agree to join you, then?"

Julie's tone was dry, and he looked slightly shamefaced. "I hoped you would. I didn't see why you should object. After all, you have to eat, so why not with me?"

"After that enormous lunch, I could do without eating anything else today."

William seated himself on the chesterfield, in front of the fire. "You didn't eat much," he protested.

"I'm not used to eating a meal at lunchtime. I was used to having a sandwich at a coffee bar, just round the corner from the office. My main meal was in the evening."

"Well, this is only afternoon tea. You'll be hungry again by dinner time."

"Dinner time!" Julie shook her head, noticing the sandwiches and scones on the trolley, the cream cakes and chocolate biscuits, no doubt intended to stimulate William's appetite. "Do you honestly expect me to eat dinner as well!"

"Oh, sit down." William patted the couch beside him, pulling the trolley nearer and starting to pour the tea from a chunky flowered teapot. "Do you take sugar?"

"No, thanks." Julie resigned herself to the situation and sank down beside him, unfastening her boots and taking them off, toasting her toes with a ridiculous sense of wellbeing. It was cosy there, in that firelit room, sharing tea with someone who so eagerly desired her company, and she relaxed and began to enjoy herself.

They had almost finished the plate of scones when Dulcie erupted into the room. She bounced in, probably only expecting to find William in occupation, and stopped short at the sight of Julie.

"What do you want?"

William's immediate reaction was aggressive, and Dulcie stood on one leg at the end of the chesterfield, looking from one to the other of them with undisguised petulance.

"Hello, Dulcie." Julie was in a mellow mood, and decided to let bygones be bygones. "What have you been doing with yourself all day?"

Dulcie sniffed. "You're not s'posed to be in here. You're only—*staff*."

It wasn't so much the words she used as the way she said them that made Julie's hackles rise. Before she could stop herself she said, equally rudely: "If you can't say anything pleasant, keep your mouth shut!"

Dulcie was obviously taken aback, but William uttered a sound of stifled, if malicious, amusement. "She has difficulty doing that," he remarked spitefully. "It must be because of its size."

At once, Julie regretted what she had started. "Be quiet, William," she said quickly, and then: "Why don't you like me, Dulcie? My being here isn't going to make any difference to you."

Dulcie had clenched her small fists, screwed up her face into a grimace, and was glaring at William with open hatred after his verbal attack. But at Julie's words, she turned her attention to her again.

"Mummy says you're a troublemaker!" she announced scathingly. "She says you only came here because of Uncle Rhys."

"Well—I did." Julie was confused. "I am his secretary, after all—"

"That's not what Mummy means. She says you're going to try and take Uncle Rhys away from us."

"*What?*"

Julie was at once horrified at what she had heard, and alarmed to think that Nerys should discuss such things with the child.

"Don't be so stupid!" William had got to his feet and was

advancing threateningly on his cousin. "Julie's only here because *I* wanted her to come. She came because of me. She and Da don't even like one anoth—"

"Now wait a minute . . ." Julie couldn't let that go either, and she felt a reluctant sense of admiration for Dulcie who was standing her ground defiantly. "I'm here because there's a job of work to be done. All right, William—" She caught his arm, halting him. "Maybe you did influence me. But I applied for the job of my own accord."

"But you wouldn't have taken it, would you?" William looked down at her.

"That's something we'll never know," remarked a deep masculine voice behind them, and Julie turned to find her employer leaning negligently against the door frame. She wondered how long he had been there, listening to their argument, and even William seemed disconcerted. Only Dulcie was pleased to see him, and went towards him eagerly, her disappointment of the morning forgotten.

"Where have you been, Uncle Rhys?" she demanded, leaning against him, hanging on his arm. "You've been away all afternoon."

"I had—a call to make," he replied evasively, his eyes lingering with annoying intent on Julie's flushed cheeks and windswept hair. Then his expression darkened. "You've been outside, Miss Wood?" His attention switched sharply to William. "I trust *you* haven't."

"No—"

"Of course he hasn't," Julie was impatient suddenly. But she was still upset about Dulcie's insinuations. "I'm not a fool!"

"I never for one moment thought you were," drawled Rhys, with deceptive mildness. He paused before adding: "Did you enjoy getting outdoors?"

Julie ran smoothing, almost defensive hands over her hair.

86

She was aware of the dishevelled state of her appearance, and wished she had delayed William long enough to use a comb. "I finished transcribing your dictation an hour ago."

"That's not what I asked."

"I just—wanted some air, that's all."

He straightened away from the door, ignoring Dulcie's resentful pleas for attention, an expression of irritation marring his dark features. "I'm not accusing you of anything, Miss Wood. I was simply curious to hear your reactions to your surroundings."

Julie hardly knew how to answer him. Her own feelings of wellbeing were dissolving beneath the strength of his personality, and the knowledge of this made her unnecessarily abrupt.

"I have no complaints, Mr. Edwards," she responded stiffly, and was immediately aware that she had not pleased him.

With a muffled oath, he turned to leave, Dulcie clinging to his hand, but over his shoulder said briefly: "I'll see you both later—at dinner."

Julie squared her shoulders. "I'd prefer to have dinner in my room, Mr. Edwards," she said quietly.

Her words arrested him, but even as he swung round to look at her William made his objection. "You can't!" he exclaimed, in dismay. "You can't spend the whole evening in your room!"

"Miss Wood is at liberty to make her own decisions, William," remarked his father, without expression. "A secretary doesn't expect to work all day and evening as well, am I not right, Miss Wood?"

Julie opened her mouth to speak again, wanting to defend her right to choose which Rhys was somehow using against her, but William forestalled her, the familiar signs of distress quickening his breathing.

"The evenings are the worst time!" he cried, tears of frustration only narrowly restrained. "I thought—I thought we could—talk—or—or play games—"

"William! William, stop it!"

His father was getting angry with him, and Dulcie began to chant: "Willie's going to cry ... aye, Willie's going to cry ... aye .. !" at the top of her voice.

Julie exchanged one glaring look of accusation with his father, and then put an arm about William's shaking shoulders. "It's all right, William, it's all right," she soothed. "Calm down. We can talk about this . . ." But Dulcie's chanting was making talking impossible, and losing her temper, she looked up at Rhys, demanding angrily: "Can't you shut that child up?"

"I could say the same to you," he countered savagely, and Julie lost control.

"She wants putting over your knee, and giving a damn good hiding!" she declared hotly, and then felt horrified at her own audacity.

But just at that moment Nerys appeared in the open doorway, attracted, no doubt, by the noise, and the way her eyes went straight to Julie left the girl in no doubt that she had heard what had been said. Her lips tightened into a thin line, and addressing herself to Julie she snapped: "You're over-reaching yourself, Miss Wood. Dulcie is my daughter, and I'll decide her punishment, if any punishment is necessary."

Dulcie, sensing the increasing hostility, ran to her mother. "You won't let her hit me, will you, Mummy?" she cried appealingly, and watching her, Julie was sickened by the child's duplicity. Old for her years, she had immediately grasped the implications of the situation, and was using them to her own ends.

"Of course no one's going to hit you, darling," Nerys comforted her daughter, and then turned on Julie again. "How dare you upset Dulcie like this? What's been going on here? What have you said to her?"

To Julie's astonishment, and William's, too, judging by the way his breathing became a little easier, Rhys intervened. "There was a misunderstanding, Nerys. Nothing to get alarmed about. But I'm afraid Miss Wood sees herself in the role of William's protector. In any event, Dulcie was not involved, only to the extent of making a nuisance of herself."

Dulcie's face took on a sulky aspect. "Why is Uncle Rhys being horrid to me, Mummy? I didn't do anything."

Nerys controlled her own temper with obvious difficulty. Her eyes challenged those of her brother-in-law, but from Julie's point of view she could see no softening in his gaze. "I think it's a shame if a child can't behave as she likes in her own home," she said, with asperity, and Rhys inclined his head as if in agreement. "Perhaps I made a mistake, perhaps I didn't understand Miss Wood's position here. I thought she was your secretary, Rhys, not William's nursemaid."

"As you said, Nerys, it's a shame if a child can't behave as he likes in his own home," he conceded, and a faint smile began to lift the corners of her mouth. But it disappeared again as he continued: "And this is William's home, too, isn't it?"

There was absolute silence for several seconds, and then with an exclamation, Nerys swept out, taking Dulcie with her, leaving Julie feeling more embarrassed than ever. Rhys, however, seemed unaware of her feelings. He looked at his son, and just for a moment there appeared to be a glimmer of communication between them.

Then he said quietly: "I suggest you let Miss Wood make up her own mind about dinner, William. Or she may decide to leave us altogether."

But after he had gone, Julie gave in.

Not because William had been difficult. On the contrary,

he had been curiously subdued. But simply because she could not allow him to be the brunt of Dulcie's malice, as he surely would be if she did not appear. No doubt Dulcie had already told her mother what had happened, and while in one way it was possible that Nerys might despise Julie for giving in, it was much more likely if she did not join them, that Nerys would find some way to denigrate William in his father's eyes yet again.

So Julie had joined the family for dinner, and a very uncomfortable meal it was, too. Rhys was detached and unapproachable, William and Dulcie spent the whole meal making surreptitious faces at each other across the width of the table when their parents were not looking, and Nerys was coldly aloof, in her clinging gown of champagne silk jersey. Julie, who had merely changed into a simple green woollen dress with a cuffed collar, felt distinctly out of place, particularly as Rhys' wine red velvet dinner jacket matched Nerys' appearance for elegance.

When the meal was over, she escaped into the hall, and had reached the stairs when William's voice detained her. "Can I come to your room, Julie?"

He was not distressed now, not using his physical weaknesses to arouse her sympathies, yet heartrendingly appealing even so. She looked at him helplessly, aware of the responsibilities she was accepting by giving in to him, but unable to deny them.

"I—all right," she agreed, feeling a pang as the anxiety was lifted from his thin features, and he came on eagerly up the stairs behind her.

By the end of her first week at Devil's Mount, Julie felt as if she had always lived there. It was a strange thing, but her involvement with the members of this household had made her life in London assume a vagueness that usually only the passage of much time could evoke. It was difficult indeed to believe that up until a few weeks ago she had never heard of Rhys Edwards and his son when now their influence coloured her life to the exclusion of all else.

And time did not drag on her hands as she had once wondered, during those periodic bouts of uncertainty she had experienced while she was still working in London. Every morning, except Saturday and Sunday, she worked with Rhys for about four hours in the library. Although his speed of dictation did not always flow as smoothly as it had done on that first morning when the gates of inspiration had burst open, his potential output was tremendous, and his grasp of vocabulary such that there were times when her pencil moved automatically, her brain fully occupied with absorbing the tale he was unfolding.

It was a raw and brutal picture he was painting, only fleetingly interspersed with moments of descriptive gentleness. It would not be a book for the squeamish, nor for anyone merely looking for an undemanding entertainment. It was full of action and excitement, and yet the central character, Barnabas, exhibited a rare humanity, seldom found in such writing. Julie was never bored when he was dictating, always eager to know what was to happen next. And if occasionally she found her eyes dwelling rather too intently on the lean lines of his dark face, she told herself that her compulsion towards him was of a purely aesthetic nature. When they were working he was like a stranger to her, and often she wondered whether he was actually aware of her presence at all, except as a rather useful machine on which to expend his thoughts. But she was always aware of him, never more so than when whatever injury it was which had caused him to move so awkwardly at times caused a spasm of pain to cross his face, and he sought respite in the narcotic relief of a cigar. Not that she dared question his discomfort. A certain hardness around his eyes discouraged the sympathy which trembled on her tongue, and silenced the compassion inside her.

For the most part, her afternoons were taken up with transcribing her shorthand. But as soon as William had recovered sufficiently to go out again, they began taking walks in that twilight hour, before sharing tea round the living room fire, as they had done on that first afternoon. William had explained that Nerys had her own sitting room, and that until her, Julie's arrival, he had more often than not sat alone. She had not asked where his father spent his time, but she could guess.

Before coming to Devil's Mount, neither Julie nor William had spent much time in such uncultivated surroundings. They were both more used to the sights and sounds of the city than the mountainous countryside beyond the village, or the lonely, pine-clad slopes of the coastline. But their surroundings began to take a hold on them, and after becoming interested in the various types of shells and rock formations to be found below the cliffs, they began invading the library in the evenings, searching through the heavy tomes there for articles on fossils. The dusty volumes they disturbed had not been opened for years. There was even an ancient edition of Britannica. And as such information was only narrowly qualified over the years, they found enough information to make their quest interesting.

Dulcie was the one most put out by their investigations. Until now, William's world had been as limited as her own, and his unhappy associations with school had given her a feeling of superiority over him. She was not attending school herself, but William had confided to Julie that she had used to attend a small private school in London, until their move to Abernarth had curtailed all that. She could read, not well, but capably, and judging by the time she spent with her mother, could probably copy out letters reasonably well, too. Julie reasoned that she must do something. Nerys did not strike her as the kind of mother to spend too much time playing with her child.

But now, under Julie's guidance, William was entering a wider field of studies, and Julie herself was quite surprised at his aptitude for learning. She had assumed that part of his problems at school stemmed from an inability to keep up with his fellow pupils, but she soon revised that opinion. And why not? she asked herself one evening, when William was expounding on a theory of time scales which left even Julie herself groping for knowledge. His father was a brilliant man, writing with equal skill about aerodynamics, or the economic necessities of developing African communities, his use of the language a privilege to perceive. Why shouldn't his son accomplish as much, if not more, given the same opportunities to succeed. Still, that was not her concern. It bordered on that forbidden topic—personal involvement, and her only purpose was to provide the boy with something to exercise his brain.

Nevertheless, there was still Dulcie to contend with, and her intrusions into the peace of the library after dinner, were becoming increasingly frequent and annoying.

Julie knew the child ought to be in bed, though she could hardly say so. She ought not to join the adults for dinner. She was only six, after all, and a high tea around five o'clock, followed by milk and biscuits at seven-thirty, would have been more in keeping with her age. Instead of which, she ate dinner, which was seldom over much before eight-thirty, and was then allowed to play around until nine or nine-thirty, making a nuisance of herself whenever possible.

One evening, Julie and William had set out a collection of shells they had made that afternoon on the desk in the library. The night before there had been quite a storm, and in consequence the shore had been littered with debris of all kinds. They had found a dead seagull which William had insisted on burying in the sand, and several coloured feathers, suitable for using as painting utensils, but it was the shells which attracted Julie's attention. There were several rather unusual designs, which she guessed had probably been thrown up from deeper offshore waters, and William pounced on them excitedly. There were a number of whorls, one larger than the rest, pale pink, with a right-hand spiral; there was a pagoda-like object which Julie remembered reading was commonly found off the shores of Japan, although this was probably nothing so exotic; and a frilled oyster shell, coloured almost purple. These were their prime specimens, but they had collected a number of commoner varieties, many of which were delicately coloured and would polish to a high gloss. They were in the process of identifying the different molluscs who had made their homes in the shells when Dulcie burst into the room.

She never knocked, and this evening there was a high colour in her cheeks as though she had already received some form of reproof. Julie speculated that perhaps she had interrupted Rhys, who she knew was reading the day's typescript in his study, a room which according to William was out of bounds to the other members of the household. All Julie knew was that the room was at the back of the house, and from their walks on the cliffs she had occasionally seen someone standing at the narrow window, watching them. But to get close enough to the windows to see inside, one would have needed to hurdle thickly-thorned bramble bushes, which were no doubt grown there for the purpose.

Now, however, Dulcie surveyed their labours with a sullen air, pursing her lips and walking across to them, scuffing her toes against the worn carpet.

"What're you doing?" she asked petulantly, and Julie put a restraining hand on William's arm when he would have risen and ordered his cousin out of the room.

"We're identifying shells," she explained pleasantly, indicating the small labels William was preparing to stick on the

94

matchboxes he had collected from Haggar and Mrs. Evans to store his collection. "Do you want to watch us? They're quite pretty."

Dulcie sniffed. "You'll get into trouble putting those things on Uncle Rhys's desk," she said. "Salt stains, Mummy said so."

Julie hid her impatience. "They're not actually on the desk, Dulcie. William's put tissue pads beneath them."

"Why don't you clear off?" demanded William, losing his temper, and causing Dulcie to make another of her faces at him.

"Now, stop that," reproved Julie, with a sigh. "This is one occasion when Dulcie could help us."

"How?"

William was suspicious and even Dulcie looked surprised.

"Well—" Julie chose her words carefully. "Dulcie could put the shells into the boxes and stick on those labels you've been writing, William."

"She couldn't—"

"Why not?"

"She'd muddle them up."

"No, I wouldn't . . ."

"I don't see why she should," exclaimed Julie, trying to be fair. "It's not a difficult job."

William hunched his bony shoulders. "I don't want her helping us," he muttered, and Julie felt a sense of sympathy with him, even while she endeavoured to befriend Dulcie.

"Look," she said, turning to the little girl and picking up a small cream-coloured specimen. "A tiny winkle—that's a small shellfish—used to live in here. Right down there inside. Isn't it pretty?"

She allowed Dulcie to hold the shell between her fingers, pointing out the striped effect that shades of a colour could create.

"Is the winkle still inside?" asked Dulcie doubtfully, keeping the shell at arm's length, and Julie smilingly shook her head.

"No. He's moved on to another home."

"Inside somebody's tummy," remarked William maliciously, and Dulcie thrust the shell away.

Julie sighed, casting an impatient look in William's direction. "Shellfish are eaten, Dulcie, you know that. You eat crab —and lobster, don't you?"

"Are they shellfish, too?" Dulcie frowned. "Do they live in shells like these?"

"Of course not, silly—"

Julie interrupted William's scathing denial, to pick up the pagoda shell, delicate in its subtle shades of blue and green. "Look at this one," she said quickly, before an argument could develop. "This is much bigger than the other. Don't you think it looks rather splendid?"

Dulcie took the shell from Julie's hands, and although Julie could sense William's tension behind her, she felt confident that the child was growing interested.

"I've not seen one like this before," she said wonderingly, poking her small finger into the cavity. "Where did you get it?"

"We found it this afternoon," replied Julie, holding out her hand to take back the shell. "Down on the rocks. It's quite unusual to find something like that. It's very rare."

"Is it?" Dulcie frowned. Then she looked up. "So it's not yours, is it?"

"What do you mean?" Julie couldn't suppress the automatic retort.

"The cliffs and the beach are private—Mummy said so. I s'pose they belonged to Daddy once, but now they belong to Uncle Rhys."

"So what?" William was abrupt.

"So this shell really belongs to Uncle Rhys, doesn't it? It's as much mine as yours. I'm going to ask him if I can keep it."

"Like hell you are!"

William was half out of his chair before Julie could stop him, snatching the shell from Dulcie's hands and holding it triumphantly out of reach. With a little scream of anger, Dulcie stood there, clenching and unclenching her fists, stamping her foot in frustration. Then, without warning, she threw out her arm and swept the collection of shells clean off the desk on to the floor, destroying all the work William had put in categorizing them, and stamping on them with her small feet before dashing out of the room.

It was an act of such magnitude in William's eyes that he just sank down into his chair, clutching the pagoda shell convulsively to him, staring disbelievingly at the jumble of debris on the floor. Dulcie's light-weight had made little impression on those shells which had landed cleanly on the carpet, but where one or more shells were crushed together, chipping and cracking had occurred. It had taken William over an hour to catalogue the few shells he had identified, and now they were all mixed together again, his labels lying useless in the general confusion.

Julie got to her feet, unsure what to do first. Should she comfort William, who had paled considerably and whose breathing was shallow and hoarse, or should she begin clearing up the mess to show him that little damage had been done? Then she saw tears rolling unheeded down the boy's cheeks, and with an exclamation she went to him, putting her arms around him, and he turned his face into her breast.

And that was how Rhys found them when he came to investigate the commotion, coming into the room with grim intent, narrowed eyes taking in the scene in one encompassing glare.

"Now what's happened?" he demanded harshly. "Is there no peace to be found in this house?"

97

"Perhaps you should ask somebody else that," retorted Julie, feeling William draw away from her to dry his eyes on the sleeve of his sweater.

Rhys surveyed the mess in the middle of the floor without expression, running one hand around the back of his neck, tugging at the hair which grew there and flexing his shoulder muscles tiredly. He had shed his jacket, and the fine silk of his shirt could not hide the darkness of the skin beneath. His actions parted the shirt at the neck and Julie's eyes were drawn to the chain of a medallion which was itself hidden, and the light covering of silver-bleached hair which clustered at the base of his throat. There was something vulnerable about him too, at that moment, and the desire to touch him, to reassure him as she had reassured William, caused a curious, but not unpleasant, pain in the pit of her stomach. Then he turned and looked at her, surprising that look in her eyes before she could hide it. His eyes were not black, as she had imagined, but slate grey, and for a second they moved with disturbing intentness to her mouth. It was a devastatingly weakening experience, almost as though he had been aware of her needs and satisfied them in the only way possible at that moment, although afterwards she blamed her overcharged emotions for imagining such a thing. Certainly, a second later he strode out of the room without a backward glance, while she was still bemused by that shattering encounter.

"Do—do you think—do you think he—he knows who did it?"

William's stammering anxiety brought her to her senses. "I don't see how he could avoid it," she answered shortly. Then: "Come on, let's start clearing up. It's not the end of the world. We can soon put them all in order again."

"But some are ruined!" exclaimed William, getting down on to his hands and knees and gathering up the broken pieces of a scallop shell.

"Well, we can find some more," said Julie, with more confidence than she was feeling right at that moment. "At least the pagoda shell is safe, although I suppose it's arguable that if you'd let Dulcie have that, the rest would have been saved."

William stared at her. "But *I couldn't*! Julie, it's mine. I found it. You don't really think I should have let her take it, do you?"

Julie wasn't quite sure what to think, but finally she shook her head. "No, I suppose not. But don't put all the blame on Dulcie, William. Children, generally speaking, reflect the attitude of their parents."

"You mean—you think—"

"I don't know what I mean," said Julie quickly, joining him on the floor and beginning to collect the unbroken shells. "Look—isn't this the one you called a leech, or something?"

William was diverted, and Julie tried to concentrate on the task in hand. But it was incredibly difficult when her thoughts kept turning to William's father. She despised herself for dwelling on that look which had passed between them when he was so obviously no amateur when it came to seducing women. He already had one illegitimate child to his credit—or discredit, whichever way you looked at it—and his own sister-in-law was panting at his heels, if not already sharing his bed. It might well amuse him to bring every female within his orbit to her knees, metaphorically speaking, especially when this particular female had allowed him to see such calflike devotion in her eyes. She felt furious with herself and furious with him, and was in no way appeased by Rhys's return with the culprit of the shell disaster.

He came into the room, holding Dulcie firmly by one small forearm, his fingers whitening the flesh laid bare by the cotton vest which together with matching pants was all she was wearing. She had obviously been hurriedly preparing for bed, perhaps to avoid any explanations to anyone, but judging by the tears streaming down her cheeks and the red marks still displayed on her bare legs, she had only succeeded in hardening her punishment. She hung her head and wouldn't look at either Julie or William, but Rhys was not about to be disobeyed.

"Well?" he said, giving her a little shake, and Dulcie lifted her face to reveal her quivering chin.

"I—I'm sorry," she choked, in an undertone, but that was not good enough.

"I want to hear what you're saying, Dulcie," Rhys told her quietly, and the deceptive gentleness of his tone was more frightening than hot anger would have been.

"I'm sorry," she said again, looking at William now, and watching her Julie could almost feel sorry for her. "I'm sorry, Willie."

William was obviously embarrassed and discomfited. He got up off the floor and muttered something like: "It's all right," in a gruff voice, going scarlet when his father looked at him.

But then of course, Julie thought wryly, as Dulcie was beginning to dry her tears, Nerys had to appear. She was surprised Nerys hadn't come on the scene before this, but Nerys herself explained this in her first words.

"I was on the phone, Rhys, and then I heard Dulcie screaming." Her eyes went disbelievingly to her daughter. "Whatever is going on? What's happened to her? And why is she only wearing her underclothes? Have you gone out of your head?"

She would have pulled Dulcie away from him, and true to type, Dulcie began to make the most of the situation. But Rhys held on to the little girl's arm, and he was perfectly calm when he spoke to her mother.

"Dulcie has just wrecked William's collection of shells, Nerys," he told her, almost pleasantly, yet with an undertone of menace. "I have administered a mild punishment, and she has just apologised for her behaviour."

Nerys did not know what to say, that was obvious. But her

eyes went straight to Julie, and she knew that this was yet another mark against her. Dulcie was crying piteously again now, begging her mother to take her away, and with an exclamation of disgust Rhys let her go. Nerys gathered the child close, successfully undoing all the good that had been done, and then looked accusingly at her brother-in-law.

"How do you know Dulcie did this?" She indicated the mess that Julie had given up trying to salvage. "Did she say so?"

"She didn't need to." Rhys folded his arms. "Unless you're suggesting that William sabotaged his own collection."

Nerys pressed her lips together. "I wouldn't put it past him."

"I saw what happened." Julie had to intervene, for William's sake. "Dulcie wanted one of William's shells. She couldn't have it, so she lost her temper. She's been punished now. I see no reason why we shouldn't all forget it."

"Oh, do you?" Nerys was sarcastic. "That's reassuring to know. You're satisfied with the results, I take it?"

"Nerys!"

Rhys spoke warningly, but Julie was determined to have her say.

"She's apologised, Lady Llantreath. I don't think you're doing the child any good by dragging every ounce of drama out of the affair—"

"How dare you?"

"—and besides, if Dulcie's really keen to have some shells of her own, I see no reason why she shouldn't accompany us sometimes on our walks."

"Do you mean that?"

From burying her face in her mother's skirt, Dulcie's disbelieving exclamation was issued through lips that still trembled, and with cheeks smeared with tears. Julie could hear William's swiftly indrawn breath, and guessed that he was horrified at her suggestion. But somehow she had to take the control of the situation away from Nerys, and she could talk to William later. He was not really a malicious boy, and if she could only make him understand that Dulcie was as much sinned against as sinning, then perhaps they would all stand a chance.

"I don't think——" Nerys was beginning contemptuously, when Rhys overrode her objections to speak to the child.

"That's not a bad offer, Dulcie," he said dryly. "I should take it up if I were you."

Dulcie's chin still quivered when she looked at her uncle. She hadn't forgiven him for administering her punishment, but her attachment to him was such that his words still had the power to influence her.

Then she looked at Julie. "You don't really mean it do you?" she mumbled, the interest in her eyes denying the indifference in her voice.

"Of course I mean it." Julie was feeling quite lightheaded with her success. Not that she was foolish enough to imagine that one skirmish meant the war was over. Nevertheless, it was a start. "We go down to the beach almost every afternoon if the weather's fine. Next time we go, you can come with us. If you promise not to be jealous if William finds more shells than you do."

"Oh, come along, Dulcie." Nerys had had enough of this. She turned to Rhys. "I don't know what game you're playing, darling, but I refuse to allow any daughter of mine to go beach-combing with a girl scarcely out of the schoolroom!"

"She's not that young, Nerys!" retorted Rhys quietly, and Julie saw the other girl's eyebrows lift interrogatively.

"No, I suppose she's not," Nerys agreed bitterly, "but those cliffs are dangerous, and so are the rocks beneath."

"Oh, but Mummy——" exclaimed Dulcie unhappily, only to be silenced by a look.

"You may not care what happens to William—" Nerys was relentless, but now Rhys intervened.

"Naturally I care what happens to William," he snapped coldly. "But I happen to believe that Miss Wood has her fair share of common sense. She's not about to do anything to risk her own life or the children's.' Besides, you're exaggerating. I played on those rocks when I was a boy, and I'm still here."

"Yes, you are, aren't you? But so am I. And I'm Dulcie's guardian, not you."

"Mummy!"

Dulcie's cry was indignant now, but Nerys paid no attention to her. Taking her firmly by the hand, she led her out of the room, and they could hear Dulcie's protests and Nerys's staccato replies until the distance between them muffled the sound.

The silence in the library after their departure was magnified by Julie's own feeling of responsibility. She had suggested the shell collecting sessions, after all, and because of her Dulcie had got her hands on the blue-green pagoda.

Then she became aware that Rhys was watching her, and she rushed into speech, anything to dispel the tension on the atmosphere.

"I—I suppose I—I'm to blame," she stammered unsteadily. "I in—invited Dulcie to join us. I sh—showed her the shells. If I hadn't she would eventually have gone away and left us alone."

"It wasn't your fault," began William, but his father cut him off.

"You were right about Dulcie," he said, looking at Julie with that narrow-eyed stare she found so disturbing. "She does need more discipline—I should have realised it before. Only I'm afraid I was involved with other things." He paused, and a certain cynicism twisted his lips. "I'm sure Dulcie will enjoy grubbing around the rocks, though, as you and William do. All —children enjoy that sort of thing."

The hesitation before the word "children" was deliberate, Julie felt, but right now she was more concerned with what he had said, rather than the way he said it. "But I don't understand," she murmured. "Her—mother said—"

"Leave Dulcie's mother to me," replied Rhys briefly, and Julie saw William's lips tighten at his words. Then his father nudged the jumble still lying on the floor with the toe of his suede boot. "I'll have Haggar clear this up in the morning. I should leave it for tonight. It's time you were in bed, isn't it, William?"

William hunched his shoulders. "If you say so," he said, without looking up, and Julie felt a sense of frustration. Suddenly everything had gone horribly wrong, and she just wanted to escape to her room until her treacherous emotions subsided.

"Then—I'll say goodnight," said Rhys quietly, turning towards the door. "Goodnight."

Both Julie and William made a polite rejoinder, but after his father had gone, William flung himself bitterly into the leather armchair.

"Did you hear that?" he demanded fiercely. "We're going to be stuck with Dulcie after all. Why on earth did you invite her?"

"We'll talk about it tomorrow," said Julie, more calmly than she felt, particularly, as her own reasons for not welcoming the news had nothing to do with Dulcie herself. They had to do with Nerys—and Rhys; and whatever was between them . . .

CHAPTER SEVEN

As if the weather was determined to add its own disapproval to the plans, the next few days were wet and stormy. The afternoon walks, which Julie and William had so much enjoyed, had to be curtailed, and when she finished typing for the day Julie spent some minutes sitting on the window seat in the library, staring out at the dreary scene which confronted her, before joining William in the living room.

At night, the noise of the sea surging greedily over the rocks below the cliffs made sleeping difficult, and one night Julie was awakened by a shattering crash below her windows. Her brain, refreshed by its brief period of unconsciousness, was sharp and alert, and she sat up in bed anxiously, not quite sure what she should do. She wasn't really frightened, although the sound itself and her sudden awakening had set her heart hammering in her chest, but the idea of going downstairs to investigate was still a daunting one.

Nevertheless, someone had to discover what had happened, and as the sound had come from below her windows, she guessed a window in the dining-room had been broken. How?—she did not care to speculate.

Pulling on the soft cream jersey robe which had been her mother's last birthday present to her, Julie pushed her feet into her mules and crossed to the door. Outside, on the balcony above the shadowy hall, there was no sound at all, and she wondered fleetingly whether she had dreamed the whole thing. The temptation to return to her bed was strong, particularly as it was cold out here on the landing, but her conscience would not let her. If a window was broken and it rained before morning, the dining-room would be in an awful mess.

The wind was howling eerily as she descended the stairs, and her vivid imagination quickly transposed her surroundings to those of a castle in Saxon times, and she, the maiden of the house, alone and undefended, was facing the invasion of Viking intruders.

She neared the bottom of the stairs. There was sufficient light from a moon, occasionally hidden behind scudding clouds, to illuminate her passage, but in any case she would have been loath to reveal her presence until she was sure she was alone.

The soft pad of footsteps suddenly froze her to the bottom stair. There was something stealthy about the sound, and her heart rose suffocatingly into her throat. What if she had been mistaken? What if what she had assumed to be the wind had been really an intruder? She ought not to have come down here without alerting some other member of the household, Rhys Edwards for example, but she realised in those fleeting seconds that she didn't even know where he slept.

Clouds thickened at that moment, plunging the hall into darkness, but when the dining-room door opened, she could see the silhouette of a man illuminated clearly against the uncurtained windows of the room beyond. The figure was tall and broad, curiously attired in some long robe, and a sob escaped her. This must all be some crazy nightmare, she thought wildly, pressing a hand to her lips, convinced beyond reason that the figure before her was the Viking of her imagination. She gulped and turned to flee, driven without quite knowing why, and then halted abruptly when the hall was suddenly flooded with light.

"For God's sake! *Julie!* What the hell are you doing down here?"

Julie turned reluctantly to face her employer, her eyes widening as she took in his appearance. The robe which had frightened her so was a long poncho-like garment, magnificently embroidered with threads in gorgeous colours along its hem, wooden toggles holding the two sides together. It was, she guessed, of African origin, and revealed between the side toggles that he wore nothing beneath it.

Her face suffused with colour at this knowledge, although he seemed less concerned with his appearance than by hers.

"Well?" he asked impatiently. "I suppose you heard the crash."

Julie nodded. "I thought it might be—a window."

"It was." Rhys indicated the room behind him. "I'm going to have to seal it up somehow until the morning. The rain's coming in."

"Oh? Is it raining?"

It was a silly conversation to be having in the early hours of the morning, but Julie couldn't think of anything else to say. Her palms were moist, and she was having difficulty in avoiding looking at him, her eyes drawn to the unfamiliar sensuality of his attire. On anyone else, she conceded, it might have looked improper, or theatrical, but on Rhys it was entirely acceptable.

Now he was regarding her with ill-concealed impatience. "You can go back to bed," he told her quietly. "There's nothing you can do."

But even as he spoke, he uttered a muffled oath, and twisted one bare foot upward so that he could see the sole. Julie saw the splinter of glass that was causing his discomfort almost before he did, and stepping off the last stair, said quickly: "Let me do that."

"No." His hand warded her off, and she looked at him helplessly.

"Why not? You might break it. It's very dangerous to risk having slivers of glass floating round inside you."

"A most unpleasant possibility," he agreed mockingly. His eyes moved slowly over her, taking in the rounded curves of her body, tantalisingly accentuated by the clinging robe. "Go back to bed, Miss Wood. You're no Androcles!"

Julie held the lapels of her gown closer about her throat. "I could say, you're no lion, Mr. Edwards!" she declared.

"Oh, but I am," he retorted harshly. "And if I were you, I'd go back to bed before you catch your death of cold!"

With one hand supporting himself on the banister, he pulled impatiently at the splinter. Blood surged below the skin as it moved, but it was deeply embedded, and it snapped between his fingers, leaving a shred of glass still lodged in his foot.

His expression was not encouraging as he looked at her, almost as if he blamed her lingering presence for what had occurred. Then his lips tightened.

"I'm afraid I'm going to have to take you up on that offer, Miss Wood," he said shortly. "I just hope you're not squeamish."

Blood was dripping from his foot on to the wooden floor and she watched it, mesmerised, for a moment, before saying jerkily: "I—is there somewhere we can use?"

"The kitchen," he decided abruptly, and limped off across the hall, using his heel for support.

Julie had only briefly entered Mrs. Evans' domain, but at night it was warm and comfortable, the artificial light glinting on the shining cooker and the pans hung on the wall, evidence that in this area at least, Mrs. Evans was not lacking.

"There's a medical cabinet around here somewhere," muttered Rhys, opening and closing cupboard doors, unable to find any of the things he wanted.

"Look," said Julie at last, "don't you have some alcohol of some kind? I should have thought that you—that is—well, not everybody has a convenient medicine chest," she finished uncomfortably.

Rhys regarded her strangely. "What has William been telling you about me?" he demanded. "What secretive little conversations do you have on those walks of yours? No wonder he was against Dulcie accompanying you. She tells tales, as I'm sure you've gathered. It would be awkward having to explain your opinions to me, wouldn't it?"

"You flatter yourself!" declared Julie hotly, stung by his bitter sarcasm. "William and I have more interesting topics to talk about than you!"

He turned from examining the contents of a shelf above the draining board, and he was closer than Julie had realised. She stepped back, aghast at her own temerity, and her expression brought his mouth into a thin line.

"Perhaps we should conduct all our conversations at night, Miss Wood. At least then I could be sure of hearing the unvarnished truth!"

Julie flushed. "I'm sorry."

He shook his head angrily. "Don't be. I asked for that." He turned back to the shelf again. "There's nothing here. You find something to take the splinter out with, and I'll get the alcohol."

Julie doubted there was anything suitable here with which to extract glass, and the idea of using a knife did not appeal to her. Rhys had gone to his study to get a bottle, and after a moment's hesitation she left the kitchen herself and ran upstairs to her room to collect her manicure set. There were some tweezers in there which might be suitable, and if not, perhaps he could think of something else.

Rhys was waiting in the kitchen when she returned, and his eyes narrowed as he took in her breathless appearance. "Where have you been?"

She showed him the manicure set, recovering rapidly, and he nodded before asking where he should sit.

"Perhaps on the table would be best," she suggested, looking up at the single bulb which was suspended in the middle of the room. "The light is better there."

Rhys shrugged, and levered himself on to the scrubbed surface of the table, waiting patiently while she unstoppered the bottle of Scotch and applied a little to a clean handkerchief she had taken from her pocket.

"You don't want me flat on my back, do you?" he enquired, half amused by the seriousness of her expression, and Julie's colour deepened again.

"If—if you could just rest your foot across your knee," she suggested tentatively, and obediently he complied.

She was overwhelmingly aware of his nearness, and as she bent her head to examine the wound, the warm odour of his body filled her nostrils. The skin of his sole was hard as though he was not unused to going barefoot, but it was bloodstained now, and she had to clean this away before tackling the splinter. Her handkerchief was soon a grimy rag, splashed with crimson in places, and she took it to the sink and rinsed it thoroughly in cold water before continuing. The alcohol she applied to the cloth must have stung abominably, but apart from a certain tautness about his features, he made no demur. It was an odd sensation, touching him like this, particularly as the scarcity of their attire made the situation that much more intimate.

The splinter was lodged in the flesh that thickened the pad below his toes, and because of its situation bled profusely every time she attempted to move it. Julie could feel her teeth digging into her lower lip as she concentrated on the task, but a certain sense of inadequacy invaded her efforts. His skin was too tough. If she used the tweezers and attempted to withdraw the shred of glass, it would simply break again, making its extraction that much more difficult.

"You'll have to use a knife," observed Rhys dryly, just above her head, and she looked up at him with startled eyes.

"What?"

"It's the only way," he told her flatly. "You're going to have to open it up."

Julie looked down quickly so that he should not see her expression, but a feeling of revulsion was filling her at the thought of using a knife on his flesh. She couldn't do it, she thought wildly. She would be sick!

"What's the matter?" There was a trace of irritation in his tone now. "I shouldn't have thought you'd have experienced any qualms at the idea of cutting me up. Or is the whole idea just distasteful to you?"

"That's not fair!" Julie twisted the handkerchief between her fingers. "I—I've never done anything like that before."

"Just think of all the occasions I've been cruel to William," he remarked mockingly. "That should give you more satisfaction."

She looked up at him indignantly. This close she could see the length of his thick lashes, the brown pores of his skin, the uneven whiteness of his teeth. She had been close to members of his sex before, but never to one who disturbed her as this man did. He aroused the most wanton thoughts inside her, and her imaginary skirmishes with her Viking were as nothing compared to the emotions she was experiencing now.

As if aware of her desire for contact with him, he put out a hand, his hard fingers closing over hers. "What's the matter, Julie?" he asked, reverting to the way he had addressed her when she had surprised him in the hall. "Are you squeamish, after all?"

"I—why—*no!*"

Her breathing had quickened to a considerable degree and her eyes dropped before the penetration of his. His hand holding hers fascinated her, lean and brown and long-fingered, faintly covered with fine dark hair. She was trembling, and realising he must be aware of this, too, she tried to free herself.

But he would not let her go, and hardly knowing what she was doing, she pressed both hands to her chest. His knuckles were hard against her breast, and she quivered violently when one long finger probed the lapels of her robe, seeking and finding the hardened nipple outlined against the soft material.

Then, with an impatient exclamation, he withdrew his hand, thrusting both feet to the ground and standing up. "Go to bed, Julie!" he muttered, and she knew he was angry now, but whether with her or with himself she could not be sure.

"I—your foot . . ." she stammered helplessly, and was reduced to silence by the look in his eyes.

"I can do it," he told her, with cold emphasis. "Go to bed, Julie, and don't ever let any man do that to you again, not unless he intends more than a selfish experiment!"

Julie licked her dry lips, unable to leave without knowing the truth. "And—and was that your intention?" she asked unsteadily.

"My—intention?" Rhys brushed past her to take a knife from the rack hanging on the wall beside the cooker. It was a vicious-looking weapon, with a narrow, sharp-pointed blade. "I'm a man, Julie, and for years I've been used to taking what I want when I want it. You know—or you may have guessed, it doesn't matter which—that I've lived in Africa, lived by rules you wouldn't begin to understand. You have a beautiful body, and you arouse me. What do you think my intention was?"

Julie couldn't stop shaking. Her knees were knocking, and she prayed he couldn't hear them.

He halted before her, the knife hanging loosely from his hand. The primitiveness of his attire combined with the darkness of his skin reminded her of his alien background, but the core of excitement inside her was not motivated only by fear.

"Well?" he said grimly. "What are you waiting for? Surely you've heard enough about me by now to know that I have little respect for anything or anyone."

"I've heard nothing about you," she denied swiftly, wrapping her robe more closely about her.

"No? And of course, you've never speculated." His lips twisted. "Forgive me if I find that hard to believe."

"What am I supposed to have heard about you?"

He uttered a short laugh. "Ask Nerys. She'll be only too willing to oblige." Then he cast a wry look towards the ceiling. "Which reminds me, she'll be wondering why I've been so long ..."

Julie gulped sickeningly. His words, and the mocking glint in his eyes, struck through the cloak of intimacy she had been consciously weaving about them. The wind whistling outside, the warmth of the kitchen, attending to his injury—all these things had brought her closer to him, had aroused an emotional response which in the cold light of day she would despise herself for. And now he had put into words the suspicion which she had nurtured for the past three weeks, and she hated him for it.

She took a jerky step backward, away from him, and came up against the edge of the table. "Then perhaps you should get her to take the glass out of your foot," she got out tightly.

"Nerys wouldn't soil her hands on anything so coarse," he retorted abruptly. "Oh, go away, Julie, before I change my mind."

"Change your mind?"

"Yes," he muttered, through clenched teeth. "Change my mind! About—this—"

And dropping the knife to the floor, he reached out and put his hands on her hips, drawing her resisting body towards him.

Julie's hands against his chest were no great barrier to overcome, and when her thighs encountered the muscled hardness of his, her own body betrayed her. She looked up at him through startled eyes and saw the darkening emotion in his eyes before his mouth descended on hers. If he had been brutal with her, she would have fought him all the way, but instead his mouth moved softly and caressingly over hers. He held her closely, his arms supporting her as weakness invaded her legs and made it impossible for her to draw away. Then he parted her lips, and the hardness of his mouth brought an upward surge of sweetness flooding her being. She was drowning in sensual feeling, vertiginous, oblivious to everything but the thrusting urgency that made her cling to him, her sleeves falling back as her bare arms wound themselves round his neck. She knew what she was inviting, but for once in her life she was without the will, or the desire, to resist.

"Julie!" he groaned hoarsely, more aroused than he could cope with, burying his face in the thickening glory of her hair, stroking her shoulder laid bare by his questing hands.

To the boy standing in the doorway, his face waxen-pale in the artificial light, they must have looked pagan and abandoned, intent only on the satisfaction of their senses, entirely wrapped up with one another, uncaring who could see them.

Julie saw him first, over his father's shoulder, and something inside her wept for the despairing look she could see on his face.

"William!" she gasped, when Rhys would have possessed himself of her mouth again, and the word tore them apart more thoroughly than any douche of cold water could have done.

Pushing her almost roughly away from him, Rhys turned, his son's name on his lips, but the doorway was empty. William had gone.

"Are you—"

"Sure? Yes, of course I am," she gulped chokingly, fastening the belt of her robe around her. "He was there!"

"*God!*"

Rhys limped across the room, and she took a couple of uncertain steps after him. "Where are you going?"

The look he turned on her was enough, and she made a helpless gesture with her shoulders. "Your ... foot ..."

"To hell with my foot!" he retorted savagely, and strode out of the room.

Back in her room, Julie climbed wearily into bed. She was cold now, cold and miserable, sick with the realisation of what she had done. For there was no doubt in her mind that she had been to blame—for everything. If she had gone back to bed, either when first he suggested it in the hall, or later after she had been unable to use the knife on his foot, none of this would have happened, and now she strained her ears to hear any sounds from William's room further along the hall.

But outside the sea was lashing itself into a fury on the rocks below, and the crying of the wind through the eaves was human enough to disguise any other sounds which might be heard. Julie had never listened to the forces of nature released with such elemental violence, and she buried her head under the pillows, as much to hide from the world in general as to escape the angry force of the storm.

Not that she could hide, or close her ears, to the contempt she felt for herself and for the man who could come from one woman's bed and show himself capable of possessing another. She had never been so close to a man before, and even now, contemptuous as she was of her own weaknesses, she could not completely dispel the treacherous needs he had aroused inside her. Despite what she felt was a modern outlook, she was, like many girls of her age, more experienced in the theoretical practices of sex than the physical ones. She had not known she could feel the way she was feeling now, but the remembrance of his hard body against hers could still bring a yielding lethargy to her bones.

Oh, *God*, she thought sickly, rolling on to her stomach, burying her face in her pillows, if William had not appeared in the doorway, what might she have done...?

The wind was abating, and the faint light of morning was

probing her curtains before Julie fell asleep, but then only fit-fully, aware that somehow she had to get up and behave as though nothing had happened in a couple of hours. And not for her sake—but for William's.

She did not dare to speculate on what his reactions to last night's scene might be. What had his father said to him? What explanation had he given, if any, and how could anyone excuse their behaviour? What if Rhys asked her to leave? What if he decided it would be the best thing for all of them if he employed the older woman he had intended in the first place? Why did that prospect fill her with such dismay? Because, in these few short weeks, she had begun to care for William in a way that made the idea of leaving him again almost impossible to contemplate.

She dressed in slim-fitting jeans that flared at the ankle and a navy knitted shirt, and as she did so, she considered whether she should try to speak to William herself before breakfast. But although she went along to his room, there was no sound from within, and she did not have the courage to turn the handle and walk in. Besides, she justified her timidity, he could still be sleeping. He had had a disturbed night, after all.

She breakfasted alone in the dining room. Someone had swept up the glass and nailed a board across the gaping pane which the wind had smashed the night before. Julie wondered if Rhys had done it himself, or whether it had been Haggar who had discovered the mess on his morning rounds.

As she ate her toast and drank her coffee—she had been unable to face anything heavier—she tried to compose what she would say to Rhys when she saw him again. She wondered what explanation he had given Nerys when he finally returned to her, and this, more than anything else, made Julie face facts. Somehow she had to show Rhys that what had happened between them meant nothing to her, that it would never happen again—and later, convince William of the same.

The library was deserted when she positioned herself at her desk at nine o'clock, and despite the heat of the fire which Haggar had laid for them, a clammy chill descended upon her. Rhys had always been there before her, had always been waiting for her on her arrival. His absence put the spectre of her dismissal more sharply into focus.

Refusing to accept that possibility, she honed her pencils to a sharper point, and opened her notebook in readiness. Ten past nine. Perhaps he had gone to see William. Or perhaps he was still with Nerys ...

Getting up from her chair, she moved across to the windows. The aftermath of the storm had left the grounds around the house littered with broken twigs and branches, leaves spread like confetti across the grass. The sea this morning was a slate grey in colour. *Slate grey* ...

She turned round abruptly, and as she did so, the door opened and Rhys himself came into the library.

Immediately Julie wished she was sitting down doing something, *anything*, rather than appear anxious at his non-appearance. Instead of which, she stood uncertainly in the window recess, waiting for him to say the words of dismissal she had convinced herself were inevitable. In black suede pants, and a black silk shirt, he had the sombre countenance of an executioner, and she could not believe he had anything good to say to her. But he was no less attractive than he had been the night before, and she wondered how Nerys could hope to hold a man like him without even the frail obligation of a wedding ring.

"I'm late," he said, non-committally, walking towards the desk. "I'm sorry, but I had to ring the glazier to come and attend to that pane of glass in the dining-room."

Julie's breath escaped noisily, and recovering herself she walked quickly to her chair and sat down. "That's all right," she managed huskily, picking up her pad.

Rhys regarded her bent head for a few moments, and then he said, half angrily: "I have no intention of apologising, you know."

Julie's head jerked up, her cheeks crimson. "I never suggested you should."

"And you're not about to offer me your resignation?"

Julie drew a trembling breath. "Is that what you want?"

His eyes narrowed. "No." He paused. "I have no complaints about your work."

"Then—then shall we get on?"

He sighed. "Very well." Another pause. "It won't happen again."

"No."

"You appreciate that?"

"Of course." Julie found there was a definite ache at the back of her throat now, and her eyes felt absurdly tight. "Is—I—was William all right?"

"Only time will tell," he replied quietly. "So we'll continue, shall we? I want to change the last two pages of typescript. I don't like that scene with Harriman."

Julie determinedly put her own feelings aside, and concentrated all her attention on the novel, and when Nerys interruped them almost two hours later, they were both engrossed with dictation.

"Rhys!" she called, from the doorway. "The glazier's here. Will you speak to him?"

Uttering an oath which only Julie overheard, Rhys threw down the fountain pen he had been twisting between his fingers as he dictated, and strode irritably towards the door.

"Where is he?"

"In the dining room, darling. His name's Meredith, Gavin Meredith—"

"I know what his name is, Nerys," retorted Rhys shortly, and passed her without another word.

After he had gone, Nerys lingered in the doorway, raising her dark eyebrows at Julie. "I wonder why he's in such a bad mood this morning," she murmured interrogatively.

"I don't know . . ." Julie wished she would go.

"That was quite a storm we had last night, wasn't it?" Nerys persisted softly. "Annoying about the dining room window. Did you hear anything, Miss Wood?"

Julie looked down at her notepad, pretending to correct her shorthand. "I heard the window break, yes," she said.

"It must have been quite eerie," Nerys mused thoughtfully. "I'm glad I don't sleep at that side of the house." She paused. "William was disturbed, too, you know. Rhys had to go down and investigate."

So that was what he had told her! Julie despised him for using his son in that way.

"I—storms don't bother me," she said at last, realising that Nerys was waiting for her to say something.

"Well, I don't like them," said Nerys, wrinkling her small nose. "Broken windows, broken glass! It's dangerous! I've told Dulcie to be sure and keep her shoes on today. Rhys got some glass in his foot last night, when he came down to investigate the crash."

Julie wished Nerys would shut up. She didn't want to be reminded about last night. She didn't want to wonder whether Nerys was not simply playing with her, taunting her, knowing the truth of what had happened. What if Rhys had told her? What if he had bragged that she had practically thrown herself into his arms? What if they had laughed about it together?

"Glass can be dangerous," Nerys was saying now. "Haggar had to get it out for him with a knife this morning. I couldn't have done it? Could you?"

Julie shook her head, and at that moment, Rhys called her. "Miss Wood! Miss Wood! Can you come here for a minute?"

Breathing a sigh of relief, Julie got to her feet and hurried out of the room, passing Nerys with a slight smile. Somehow, she did not think Nerys did know the truth of what had happened the night before, but she was astute enough to realise that it was not inconceivable that Julie might have gone to investigate the crash, too. She was probing, that was all, satisfying herself that what Rhys had told her was true.

Rhys was standing in the dining room with a tall, fair-headed young man, dressed in a denim shirt and jeans, a patched leather jacket hanging from his shoulders. The stranger looked with evident interest at Julie, and she liked his square, good-looking face, the twinkle in eyes as clear and blue as the sea on a sunny day.

"Gavin Meredith," said Rhys abruptly, intercepting their smiling exchange. "My secretary, Miss Wood."

"Julie Wood," said Julie determinedly, and Gavin's grin deepened.

"Hello, Julie."

Rhys's expression hardened. "When you've finished with the pleasantries, I'd like you to go and tell Mrs. Evans that there'll be one extra for lunch. I want—him to go over all the windows while he's here and check for possible weaknesses. I don't want a repetition of what happened last night."

Julie's eyes encountered the cold greyness of his, and she nodded her head. "Yes, Mr. Edwards."

Her deliberately formal use of his name set him apart from herself and the young glazier, but she couldn't stop herself. After her recent conversation with Nerys, she felt raw and vulnerable, and for some reason she had to prove to herself that he was not as indifferent as he seemed. But she aroused no reaction that she could see, and with a feeling of impotency, she left them.

When she came back, Rhys had disappeared, and only Gavin Meredith was crouched on his haunches, taking tools out of a canvas holdall. He grinned when he saw her, however, and straightening said:

"I haven't seen you here before."

The desire to be friendly had dissipated somewhat now that Rhys was not there to bait, but Julie was seldom impolite, and she said now: "No. I've only been working here a few weeks."

"I haven't seen you about the village either," he said, his accent soft and lilting, making his voice a pleasure to listen to. There were no undercurrents here, and Julie found herself relaxing.

"Actually, I haven't been into the village yet," she confessed, and as she did so realised that since coming to Devil's Mount, she had had neither the time nor the inclination to do so.

"Don't you have any time off?" he exclaimed, shedding his leather jacket, and she shrugged.

"I suppose I do. But there isn't a lot to do around here, is there?"

"There is if you know where to look for it," he replied, his eyes frankly admiring. "I've got a motor-bike. Would you come out with me some time?"

"You don't waste any time, do you?" she laughed, feeling the tension of the last few hours seeping away from her.

"No." He looked at her steadily. "I may not get another chance for months."

"Then I'll have to break another window, won't I?" she teased, enjoying the exchange.

"No need to do anything so drastic." Gavin was watching her closely. "My number's in the book. There are telephones here, aren't there?"

"I suppose so."

Julie smiled. All her life she had been used to boys trying to make dates with her. Some she had accepted, some she had not. It was not a unique situation. What was unique was the realisation that suddenly he seemed so young, so immature. A boy instead of a man.

"How much longer do you intend to be, Miss Wood?"

Rhys's cold voice from just behind her brought all the tension flooding back again, and the eyes she turned to his face were frankly anxious.

"I'm sorry," she murmured inadequately, and Gavin turned back to his bag of tools.

But as she followed Rhys into the library, she was conscious of Gavin's eyes following her.

CHAPTER EIGHT

JULIE'S first intimation that all was not well between herself and William came at lunchtime.

Since his recovery, he had usually come to the dining room to take his lunch. Most days, Nerys and Dulcie joined them, too, and occasionally Rhys, although often he satisfied himself with a sandwich taken in his study. But today only Dulcie came to sit with Julie at the long dining table, and the absence of anyone else left neither of them with much choice but to talk to one another.

Since the incident with the shells, Dulcie had been perceptibly less hostile towards both Julie and William, keeping out of their way as much as possible, and indicating by her frequent grimaces at the weather that she was expecting Julie to take up her promise of allowing Dulcie to accompany her and William on their next outing.

When it became apparent that no one else was going to join them, Julie suggested that they should begin. Mrs. Evans had left a steak and kidney pie in the middle of the table, and the serving dishes around contained potatoes and other vegetables. Dulcie made no demur when a plate of the delicious smelling pie was put in front of her, and she helped herself to peas and carrots.

"Mummy's gone to Llantreath," she volunteered, while they were eating, although truth to tell Julie was not particularly hungry. "Have you been there?"

Julie shook her head. "No. Have you?" Her response was automatic, her thoughts with William, wherever he might be.

"Only once." Dulcie was unaware of any abnormality in the situation. "But I couldn't go today. Mummy's going to the hairdressers, and I hate waiting around for her."

Julie heard her last few words and hoped a nod would suffice in reply. She was not really listening to her, but she couldn't help thinking how much more this conversation would have meant if William had been there, too, to hear it.

"The rain's stopped," Dulcie said, a few moments later, obviously getting round to the point of this attempt at amicability. "Will you and William be going for a walk this afternoon?"

The unconscious appeal in her voice got through to Julie, and she endeavoured to respond to it. After all, it was not Dulcie's fault this time that William had been hurt, and just because she was all mixed up inside there was no reason to go back on her word to the child.

"I—we might be," she managed at last, and Dulcie's eyes brightened.

"Can I come?"

Julie sighed. Then she nodded. "I don't see why not. Providing your mother doesn't object."

"Oh, Uncle Rhys spoke to Mummy. She won't mind," said Dulcie confidently. She paused. "But where is William?" Suspicion clouded her expression. "He hasn't gone with Mummy and Uncle Rhys, has he?"

Julie's lips parted. "I—Uncle—Rhys—has gone with your —mummy?"

"To Llantreath. Yes, I told you." Dulcie was sulky.

Julie put down her knife and fork. "Well, perhaps William has gone with them, after all." But she didn't really believe it.

"He wouldn't!" Dulcie pursed her lips petulantly. "Uncle Rhys wouldn't take William and not me!"

"But you just said that your mother was going to the hairdressers and you didn't like hanging about, waiting for her," pointed out Julie patiently.

"I know, I know. Because Uncle Rhys said he had some

business to attend to and wouldn't have time to look after me. But if William's gone, he won't be waiting at the hairdressers, will he?"

"Your Uncle Rhys is William's father, Dulcie," said Julie quietly. "Don't you think they deserve some time alone together?"

Dulcie's knife scraped nerve-rackingly across her plate. "Why? Why? I don't even have a daddy."

"William doesn't have a mummy," Julie reminded her steadily. "I'm sure William wouldn't mind you sharing his daddy, but you try to monopolise him."

"Mono—mop—what does that mean?"

Julie half smiled at her futile attempts to say the word. "Monopolise? It means to—be selfish with, to keep for yourself. Without allowing anyone else to share."

"Uncle Rhys doesn't love William."

"You don't know that."

"I do, I do!" Dulcie pushed out her chin. "He's always grumbling about him and saying that he should be in school."

"That doesn't mean he doesn't love him!"

Dulcie regarded her sourly. "Uncle Rhys doesn't say things like that to me."

"Because you're so much younger, Dulcie. You're still a little girl. William is a teenager. Naturally, his father treats him differently, but that doesn't mean he thinks any the less of him. Of course he thinks that William should be in school. Because he wants him to get a good education, maybe even go to university, have the chance of a good career. It's because he cares for him that he gets angry with him, don't you see?"

Dulcie absorbed this with evident reluctance. "Well, Mummy said Uncle Rhys had no time for William. She said he only got him out of the home because William's mummy might have tried to get money out of him later on."

Julie was horrified at the child's grasp of the situation. She must have been told this, or heard it, many times for her to recite it so accurately. Poor William! Poor Dulcie!

"Well, perhaps Mummy made a mistake," she comforted the little girl now. "People do, you know, even mummies."

Dulcie hunched her small shoulders. "Why did my daddy have to get killed?" she muttered tearfully. "I want my daddy!"

Julie quickly removed the dinner plates and opened a serving dish to display a cream-covered trifle. "Oh, look!" she exclaimed, with deliberate emphasis. "Fruit and jelly and sponge and cream . . . and lots and lots of hundreds and thousands on the top!"

Dulcie looked up, the uncertain tears drying on her cheeks. "It's a trifle!" she said, her chin still wobbling, and Julie feigned surprise.

"Is it? Is that what it is?"

Dulcie looked at her suspiciously. "You know it is."

"Do I?"

"You must have seen a trifle before."

Julie gave a mock frown. "Yes, I suppose I must. Oh, well, what do we do with it?"

Dulcie's mouth twitched, and Julie saw to her relief that she seemed to be getting over her tears. "We eat it," she asserted, now, and Julie acknowledged this with a solemn nod.

"But I couldn't possibly eat all that," she exclaimed, and Dulcie's smile appeared.

"You don't," she said, entering into the spirit of the game. "You spoon it out into a dish."

"Show me," said Julie, indicating the serving spoon, and kneeling up on her chair, Dulcie complied.

It was obvious from the amount of trifle which ended up on the tablecloth that Dulcie had seldom, if ever, done this sort of thing before, but there was nothing more satisfying to a child than plunging about in a dish of jelly, and Julie hoped Mrs. Evans would forgive her for the mess.

By the time they had eaten their trifle, it was quite late, and although Julie had intended to go and see if she could find William before beginning the afternoon's typing session, she decided she could not spare the time right now. She was afraid that Rhys might arrive back from Llantreath and find his typescript only half finished, and then, no doubt, he would assume that she had been wasting more time talking to Gavin Meredith.

Thinking of the young glazier, she glanced towards the windows, but the pane of glass had already been replaced, and there was little evidence now that it had ever been broken.

Dulcie accompanied her to the library, and stood there on one leg as Julie opened the door to go into the room.

"Will you—I mean, are you—going for a walk?" she asked awkwardly.

"Later, you mean?" said Julie.

"Well—yes."

"If it stays fine," Julie agreed doubtfully, wondering exactly what she was letting herself in for. If William had gone to Llantreath with his father and his aunt, what reaction would he have to Julie's making a friend of his cousin, particularly in his absence? And if he hadn't gone to Llantreath. . . .

"What time shall I be ready?" asked Dulcie excitedly, and Julie thrust her doubts aside. It was not in her nature to be unkind to anyone, least of all a child.

"I should be finished by about half past three," she said, and Dulcie went skipping away, obviously delighted at the unexpected treat.

As it happened, Julie was finished typing soon after three. The delay in starting that morning, Rhys's desire to alter a scene she had typed the previous day, plus the interruption caused by the glazier, had all contributed to a briefer output, and consequently she completed transcribing her notes in record time.

Leaving the library, she made her way to the kitchen, and found Mrs. Evans seated comfortably in her armchair by the fire, drinking tea and talking to the young glazier who was perched familiarly on the edge of the table, a mug of tea steaming in his hand, too. They both looked surprised at Julie's intrusion, and Mrs. Evans got up out of her chair to say: "Is there something I can get you, miss?"

Julie, conscious of Gavin Meredith's blue eyes upon her, felt rather uncomfortable. Smiling apologetically, she said: "Actually, Mrs. Evans, I just wanted to ask you if you knew whether William went to Llantreath with his father."

Mrs. Evans shook her head. "Oh, no, miss. William hasn't gone out, not that I know of. I took him his lunch up at about half past twelve, and Mr. Edwards had already left then."

"I see." Inwardly Julie trembled. She had suspected this, of course, but she had hoped. . . . "Well—thank you, Mrs. Evans."

"Will you stay and have a cup of tea now you're here, miss?" suggested the housekeeper amicably. "It's no trouble . . ."

"Oh, no. Thank you again." Julie shook her head, and was aware that Gavin's eyes had never left her face although she had deliberately avoided looking at him.

"Dulcie tells me you're taking her walking this afternoon," said Mrs. Evans, as Julie walked towards the door.

"Yes." Julie half turned.

"She'll enjoy that," went on the housekeeper, and Gavin slid off the table and placed his empty mug on the draining board.

"Who wouldn't?" he commented teasingly, and Mrs. Evans chuckled. She, at least, seemed to have accepted Julie's presence in the house.

Julie escaped into the hall, her cheeks rather hot, and then, without waiting for the impulse to be blunted, she ran quickly up the stairs. William's door was tightly closed, but taking a deep breath, she knocked at the panels and without waiting for a reply, opened it and went in.

William turned from his labours at a table in the window recess where he was assembling a model aeroplane. He stared across at Julie with hostile eyes, and if she had harboured any doubts about his feelings towards her, they were clarified in that moment.

"You have no right to come in here uninvited," he declared, his thin body taut within the polo-necked sweater and jeans he was wearing.

Julie closed the door and leaned back against it. "Haven't I?" She paused. "Why didn't you come down to lunch, William?"

"I wasn't hungry."

"That's not true. Mrs. Evans told me she'd brought your lunch up here."

"Oh, I see. You've been checking up on me."

Julie expelled her breath impatiently. "Don't be silly, William. I wanted to know where you were. I thought you might have gone to Llantreath with your father."

"He told you he was going to ask me then? That figures. What was it—your idea or his?"

Julie gasped. "I don't know what you're talking about. But I gather your father did ask you to go with him then."

William folded his arms. "Does that surprise you? It shouldn't. It was intended as a bribe—to ensure my silence about what I saw last night."

"*William!*"

He had the grace to colour then. "Well," he muttered defensively. "It's true."

129

"You don't know that!"

"Don't I?" In his bitterness, he was incredibly like his father. "Well, why did he invite me, then?"

"As your aunt was going along, too, I hardly think it was the action of someone wanting to hide something, do you? If he was the man you're saying he is, surely he'd avoid throwing you and Ner—Lady Llantreath together!"

William's brow furrowed. "Was Nerys going along?" He shrugged, and threw off his momentary doubt. "Oh, well, he'd know I wouldn't say anything."

"Then, by your criterion, why ask you, then?"

William's lips worked silently for a moment, then he said: "That still doesn't give you the right to come bursting in here. What do you want? I'm busy."

Julie straightened away from the door, refusing to be deterred by his insolence. "Are you coming for a walk?" she asked quietly, and his eyes flickered half remorsefully over her strained features.

"No. I've told you, I'm busy."

Julie sighed. "William, this is silly—"

"Is it?"

"Yes." She linked her fingers together. "Look, will you let me explain—"

"*No!*" He almost shouted the word. "Go away! I don't want to talk to you."

Julie took an involuntary step towards him, and then steeling herself, she halted. "Very well. If you insist on behaving like a baby, don't be disappointed if people treat you like one."

"A baby?" William was cynical. "I wish I was, do you know that? I wish I didn't understand—"

"You don't!"

"I understand that my father only has to snap his fingers for every female to jump to his bidding!"

Julie gasped. "It wasn't like that."

"Wasn't it? It looked like that to me."

"I know what it must have looked like to you, but—well, I was to blame, not him."

"Do you think that makes me feel any better?"

Julie made a helpless gesture. "I thought it might. These things happen, William. When you get a bit older, you'll understand. Men and women—they often do things that seem incomprehensible to a boy of your age." She hesitated. "It won't happen again."

"How do you know that?"

"I won't let it."

"You didn't seem to be objecting," he muttered, in a tortured voice, and suddenly she understood something much more important. He was jealous! William was jealous. But not, as she had thought, of her—but of his father!

"Oh, William!" she exclaimed, her heart reaching out to him as she stepped forward, but now he backed away from her.

"Leave me alone," he implored huskily. "I—I just want to be left alone."

"William, come for a walk."

"With you?"

"Of course with me." Julie held out her hand. "Don't stop being my friend."

William licked his lips, his eyes guarded, the colour in his pale cheeks eloquent of his upheaval. His eyes were on her face, and she wondered why she had never suspected his partiality for her company before. Perhaps because she had never seen William in that light, never realised that he was old enough to experience the first painful pangs of pubescent emotion. A sympathetic feeling of almost maternal fondness spread over her as she returned his stare, but common sense was warning her that to show her affection for him now might well precipitate a situation more complex than any she had thus far encountered.

Now William bent his head, scuffing his toe against the carpet. "Dulcie came up here," he muttered, in a low tone. "She told me you and she were going walking together. I believed her. I'm sorry, Julie."

An awful feeling of anti-climax replaced Julie's earlier elation. "Dulcie—told you that?"

"Yes. She was bragging about it, saying you'd invited her to join you. I—was—*mad!*"

"Oh, *William!*" Julie's arms swung frustratedly at her sides. What a hopelessly insecure child he was! And now she was going to have to disillusion him again. "William, Dulcie asked me if she could join us. I—I said yes."

He looked up, all the old distrust back in his face. "Did you?"

"Yes." She sighed, trying to find words to justify herself. "William, I had promised. You know I had."

"Nerys absolved you of that!"

"No, she didn't. William, can't you see, Dulcie is—like she is, because she's as insecure as—"

She broke off, but he was astute enough to guess what she had been about to say. "As insecure as *I* am?" he queried bitterly. "Don't deny it. I know that was what you were about to say. Well, now I know where I stand, don't I?"

"William—"

"Don't say any more. I don't need it, Julie. I don't need your pity. I don't need anyone."

"William, listen to me—"

"I think you've said enough."

He was absurdly adult, and she longed to gather him into her arms and comfort him as she knew she could. But that would mean another situation entirely, and one which even she dared not initiate. With a feeling of defeat, she turned towards the door. There was nothing she could say at the moment which would not sound like patronage to his ears.

As she reached for the handle of the door, his words smote an actual pain in her chest: "Enjoy your walk, Miss Wood!"

CHAPTER NINE

In fact, Julie did gain a certain release in simply getting out of the house. For days she had been confined, and it was good to free her hair from all constraint and allow the lingering breeze to tangle its silky length as she and Dulcie scrambled down the cliff path to the beach. It was fresh and invigorating down on the rocks, feeling the salty spray in their faces, wild and free by the shores of the ocean. Dulcie loved it, and for the moment Julie refrained from chiding her for taunting William. Her own emotions were still too shaken to take any more excitement.

So she gathered shells, played ducks and drakes with flat stones, and pointed out the underwater life visible in the rock pools, for Dulcie's benefit. In jeans and wellingtons and her warm parka, the little girl had never looked more animated, and Julie wished William could have been there to share it, too.

As they walked back to the house, their pockets full of the sea's bounty, Julie casually mentioned Dulcie's behaviour towards William. Without arousing any antagonism, she explained that if Dulcie wanted to share in any more outings, she should not indulge in petty spitefulness. Because of her, she said, William had been denied this outing, but in future it would be Dulcie herself who was denied if she persisted in trying to score off her cousin.

Dulcie was surprisingly acquiescent, but Julie guessed that with the least provocation that would not last. Nevertheless, the first seeds of a nicer child had been sown, and maybe they would eventually take root.

Back at the house, Rhys and Nerys had obviously returned.

There were boxes bearing the name of some Llantreath store in the hall, and the scent of expensive perfume, and Julie wondered with uncharacteristic cynicism whether her employer had been placating Nerys for his tardy behaviour of the night before.

She looked into the living room, half hoping that William might be there, but although he was not, the tea trolley was, and the smell of hot scones after the chilly air outside was very appetizing.

Dulcie had scampered off in search of her mother, eager to show her what shells they had found, and with the feeling of dejection she had felt earlier sweeping over her again, Julie went into the living room and closed the door.

The heavy chesterfield was set squarely before the fire, and shedding her coat, she went to sit down. The room was shadowy in the firelight, and she was ludicrously startled when the unseen occupant of the sofa suddenly got up from his lounging position. It was Rhys, and Julie stepped back, her heart thumping.

"I'm sorry I startled you," he said, reaching for the switch of a nearby standard lamp, and flooding their small area with an amber glow. "It was not intentional."

"Th—that's all right." Julie wrapped her arms about herself. "I—we—the trolley—"

"I know. You and William usually have tea together." His tone was coolly controlled, totally different from Julie's husky breathlessness. "It's William, actually, that I wanted to speak to you about."

"I—I thought he might be here."

"Did you? But he didn't accompany you on your walk."

"No."

"Dulcie did, though."

"Yes." Julie was defensive, but he shrugged.

"Won't you sit down?" He indicated the chesterfield.

135

Julie subsided gratefully, and after a moment he seated himself beside her, leaving the space of a cushion between them. He drew the trolley nearer, and at his silent suggestion, Julie took one of the scones, munching its crispy lightness with more determination than enthusiasm. Rhys ate nothing, she noticed, but he did pour himself a cup of tea, adding milk and two teaspoonsful of sugar.

"I've spoken to William since I got back," he said at last.

As he didn't elucidate, Julie volunteered that she had spoken to him, too.

"I know." He replaced his cup carefully in the saucer. Then: "You know what's wrong with him, don't you?"

Julie's cheeks burned. "He—he's upset. After what—what he saw last night."

"It's more than that." Rhys spoke flatly. "William has always regarded you as more his property than mine. Last night was an act of treachery, a—betrayal, if you like."

"I've told him it won't happen again!"

"Have you?" Rhys regarded her dourly. "And can you be absolutely sure of that?"

Julie almost choked on the final piece of scone, and she snatched up a napkin, hiding her face in its folds. "I think so," she answered in a muffled voice.

Rhys' mouth turned down at the corners. "Forgive me if I'm wrong, but were you, or were you not, making arrangements to meet Meredith this morning?"

Julie loved the way he said Meredith, with the emphasis on the second syllable, but she resented his interference.

"I was just talking to him," she denied hotly. "It may have slipped your notice, but I have not had any free time since I came here."

Rhys' grey eyes gave nothing away. "You're saying that I'm working you too hard?"

"I—no, not exactly."

"What are you saying, then?"

Julie bent her head. She was being unfair, and she knew it. Her hours were not arduous, and certainly time did not hang heavily on her hands. What she was talking about was the time she gave to William, and until now she had never complained about that.

"What you do in those hours when I am not employing you is your concern, Miss Wood," went on Rhys relentlessly, and Julie felt small—and mean. "If you have been giving more time to my son than you feel justified in doing, then I suggest you use this opportunity to make the break."

"What opportunity?"

Julie looked up at him apprehensively, but her stomach muscles tightened at the tenseness of his expression.

"The boy's in love with you!" he muttered harshly, flinging himself off the couch, and pacing to the windows. "Don't pretend you're not aware of it."

Julie got unsteadily to her feet, unable to sit still under such an accusation. "You're blaming me?"

Rhys turned back to her grimly, and for a moment his eyes bored into hers. Then, with characteristic honesty, he shook his head. "No," he said heavily. "No, I guess not. But that doesn't alter the situation, does it?"

Julie made a negative gesture. "I'm sorry."

Rhys nodded impatiently. "Yes. So'm I." He sighed. "So what am I going to do?"

Julie felt sick, the smell of the scones no longer an appetizing one. "You could—ask me to leave," she ventured quietly.

"I know." Rhys walked back to the hearth and stood staring into the fire, a certain weariness evident in the way he moved, and Julie wondered why both the Edwards, man and boy, should be capable of moving her so swiftly to compassion. "I have considered that."

"A—and?" The word was scarcely audible.

"I don't think that's the answer." Julie was overwhelmed by the feeling of weak relief which flooded her lower limbs at his words. "Besides," he went on, "we work well together. And I don't want to have to ask Thomas to advertise all over again." He paused. "You don't want to leave, do you?"

Something warned Julie that this was the moment she had been waiting for. How simple it would be to tell him *yes*, she had had enough, she wanted to leave. . . . But she couldn't do it. And the agony of it was, it wasn't just for William's sake that she wanted to stay!

"I—what if I said I did?" she countered, playing for time.

His expression darkened. "Do you?"

"I asked you a question."

He kicked a smouldering log further into the flames. "You're not a prisoner here."

Julie shifted from one foot to the other. "But it's not at all like—like anyone would be led to believe."

"What do you mean?" He looked at her broodingly.

"The—the advertisement—it was misleading."

"I didn't write it, Thomas did. My solicitor. He knew I wanted someone competent rather than decorative."

"But surely—the wording—it was more likely to attract—"

"Thomas is used to dealing with people. I relied on him to separate the sensation-seekers from the rest. All those I interviewed were extremely competent."

Julie linked and unlinked her fingers. "But you have to admit, this—this is hardly the home of a wealthy man."

"You don't like it?"

"I didn't say that. You *know* what I mean."

Rhys hesitated for a moment, and then with a shrug, he said: "My brother never used this place. He preferred to live in London. When I—when he died, I decided to live here. I realise it needs a lot doing to it, and right now we need someone to help Mrs. Evans with the housekeeping, but I have ideas for renovation. I'm hoping that the advance my publishers have promised me will go some way to accomplishing my plans."

"But—but—" Julie was at a loss for words. How to ask what had happened to the inheritance his brother's death must have brought him?

As if aware of her thoughts, his expression grew harsher. "I do not intend to use my brother's money, Miss Wood, even if legally it's mine. Obviously, you are aware of his identity. However, villain though I may seem, I do have my pride. Richard's money will remain intact until Dulcie is of an age to appreciate it. As for myself, I'm not quite destitute. I do have a little money of my own. But this house was my home— I love it, and I intend to keep it."

Julie felt as if she had intruded into some private grief. "I— I understand," she murmured, and in some way, she did.

Now, as though regretting his moment of confidence, he said roughly: "You, least of all the applicants, should complain of the conditions here. You came to that interview expecting a number of things which you were told had been lies. Yet you persisted in accepting the position."

"It—it must have been galling for you to have to accept me."

His lips twisted. "Are you looking for compliments, Miss Wood?"

Her nails dug into her palms. "No." She held up her head. "And—and I'll stay."

For a moment, a strange expression crossed his face, softening its lean contours, bringing a certain brilliance to his eyes, and her knees trembled violently. *She was mad*, she thought wildly, as he acknowledged her acquiescence with an inclination of his head. There was going to be nothing but trouble for her here, and she was a fool for not recognising it.

"Very well," he said now, gesturing towards the couch

again. "Please—sit down. You haven't finished your tea."

Julie sank down obediently on to the chesterfield, more than glad to take her weight off uncertain legs. Rhys did not sit down, however, but remained standing on the hearth, staring into the fire once more, as if for inspiration.

"Tell me," he said at last, "has William ever talked to you about his mother?"

Julie shook her head. "We don't discuss—personal topics."

"Your idea, I gather. William, I'm sure, would be much less circumspect." Julie said nothing and he went on: "Perhaps that's what he needs. The maternal influence—as opposed to a sexual one, hmm?"

Julie could feel a cold hand squeezing her stomach. What was coming now? Was he about to tell her that he had decided to get married? That he had asked Nerys to be his wife?

"Well?" he prompted. "Have you nothing to say for yourself?"

Julie shook her head. "It's—it's not my affair—"

"Isn't it? Don't you know that in all the best stories, this is my cue to ask you to marry me? Albeit in name only?"

Julie gasped, her teacup clattering into its saucer. Wide-eyed, she got to her feet, and encountered his sardonic stare.

"Relax!" he advised her, his voice cooler than before. "I don't have that kind of self-constraint. If I married you, you would not be able to keep me out of your bed!"

The mockery in his tone was doubly hurtful in her suddenly vulnerable condition. Pressing her palms together, she said: "I think this conversation has gone far enough, Mr. Edwards. I'm sorry about William, but I think you'll find that, given time, he'll get over any infatuation he has for me," and she moved pointedly towards the door.

"I'm delighted to hear you say so." The mockery was malicious now. "That's right. Run away, Miss Wood. Forgive me, if my words offended you. I'd forgotten—I was treating you as an adult!''

The rain returned during the following days, and in all honesty Julie could not say she was sorry. It meant that she was not put into the position of having to substitute Dulcie's company for William's, even though the extra hours spent alone in her room left too much time for thought.

William himself remained aloof from the normal workings of the household, but the fleeting glimpses she had of him revealed dark lines around his eyes, and a certain haggardness in his expression. She longed to be able to comfort him, but he avoided her eyes, seemingly determined to shun her companionship.

At least working with Rhys provided some sort of an escape. On the morning after his trip with Nerys into Llantreath, she discovered he had replaced the old chair she had been using with a black leather office chair with a revolving seat, and the knowledge that he had not forgotten his promise brought a momentary sense of foolish pride.

And working on the book had its compensations. Engrossed in the labyrinthine intricacies of the novel, Rhys became again the stranger he had once been, impersonal and detached, intent only on the satisfaction of his readers. The story had progressed through the horrors of an African military *coup* and its attendant complications, to the even more complicated power struggles going on behind the faceless masks of government. Here were all the petty intrigues she had read about in newspapers, the back-slapping insincerity of opposing factions, the creeping destruction of corruption in high places. Julie, whose reading had been limited to magazines and historical novels, found it completely riveting, and was always reluctant to call a halt for the day. The story was not moving along so quickly at the moment, there were lots of words she had to ask him to spell out for her, and places in the narrative where Rhys himself was not satisfied with its development. It was like being present at a birth, she thought in one of her more imaginative moods. A truly creative experience.

Since coming to Devil's Mount, she had managed to pen a couple of reassuring letters to her mother, which Rhys had dealt with along with his own mail. But one afternoon, finishing the typing earlier than usual, and with another letter waiting to be posted, Julie decided to walk down to the village and post it herself. She still had not seen the village, other than that brief glimpse she had had on the night of arrival, and it seemed ridiculous not to take this opportunity to stock up on a few small personal items she was also needing.

It was not a pleasant afternoon. Throughout the day there had been squally showers, but now a fine mist was settling over the headland. But it was not sufficient to deter her, particularly as it was only three o'clock, and still light enough to see her way there and back.

She put on her long boots, pulled on her tweed coat and marathon-length scarf over her working skirt and sweater, and let herself out of the house. She realised it was practically the first time she had been out alone since coming to Devil's Mount, and certainly the first time she had left the grounds.

Winding her long scarf about her neck, she tramped down the drive, pushing her mittened hands into her pockets for extra warmth. The gravel crunched under her feet, and beyond the stone gateway, the road wound desolately over the headland, making her aware of her isolation in this curiously silent world. The mist seemed to have muted even the sounds of the sea, and it was odd to be without the wind which for days had been shrieking round the house.

A bend in the road brought her in sight of the village, its roofs all one with the greyness of the small harbour below her. She could see the spire of the church, and the cottages clustered about the square, and unknowingly, her footsteps quickened. She came down the steep incline into the village, passing few people on her way, but aware of the speculative glances of those she did see. Strangers were obviously a novelty this late in the season.

The cobbled square was enclosed by the commercial premises of the village, two public houses, a general dealers, a baker's, and a post office. There were few people about here either, probably preferring the warmth of their firesides on this bleak November afternoon.

Julie decided to post her letter first, and as she hadn't any stamps, went into the small post office. Two women were talking to the postmistress when she entered, but their voices died away as they all turned to look at the newcomer. Remembering what William had said, Julie expected to see hostility in their faces, but all that was there was mild curiosity.

Approaching the counter, she waited for them to complete their business, but one of the women pulled the other aside, and said: "That's all right. We're in no hurry."

Julie smiled and asked the plump postmistress for some stamps. She was conscious of the other women watching her, however, and feeling obliged to say something, murmured: "It's a miserable day, isn't it?"

"Miserable," agreed the woman who had spoken first. "It's been a miserable week."

"Miserable," agreed the second woman, and even the postmistress echoed her sentiments.

Julie hid a smile. They were like a trio of parrots.

"You're a stranger in Abernarth?" suggested the self-appointed spokeswoman of the group.

Julie had been expecting this. "Yes." She paused. "I'm secretary to Mr. Rhys Edwards."

"At Devil's Mount?" exclaimed the second woman. "There!"

143

Julie tore off one of the stamps and stuck it on her letter. They were still watching her, and it was difficult not to fumble over her task. But she got the stamp stuck on, and put the rest of them in her purse.

"Don't you find it lonely up there?" The first woman had definitely more determination than the others. "The house was empty for so many years. Not good enough for the last owner, so I believe. I heard a rumour it was going to be sold."

"Well, I can assure you, Mr. Edwards has no intention of selling the house," said Julie firmly.

"No?" Raised eyebrows all round. "There's interesting."

Julie walked towards the door. "I must be going. I have some shopping to do before it gets dark."

"You'll know Lady Llantreath, then?" A persistent voice followed her.

Julie turned. "Yes."

"She'll be living in the house now, is she?"

Julie felt slightly impatient. "Yes."

"There! And she always said she hated it." The three women were all nodding together now. "Closed up for years, it was. After the old lady died."

Julie knew this was nothing to do with her, but something in their tone made her hesitate. It was obvious that to the people of Abernarth, Devil's Mount was something of a talking point. These people had probably known the family from way back, their relatives might well have been in service there, in the days when to work in a big house was considered quite an achievement. And they were intensely suspicious of any change in the *status quo*. William had told her that the people in the village didn't like them, but if there was a rumour going round that Devil's Mount was to be sold, it might account for a feeling of betrayal. Rhys' brother had never lived in the house after he inherited, and now that Rhys had come back, perhaps they thought it was only a matter of time before he, too, packed up and went to live in London.

"Mr. Edwards likes the house," she said now, feeling that some further reassurance was necessary. "Unfortunately, he seems to experience some difficulty in getting anyone to work there."

The three women exchanged glances. "Girls, you mean?" asked one.

Julie nodded. "*A* girl, perhaps."

"Someone to do housework, you mean?" asked another.

"Well—yes."

"I know that Mavis Jones is looking for a job," volunteered the postmistress shyly, and the other two women nodded again.

"I could have a word with her mother," said the woman who had spoken first. "A good girl, is Mavis, strong and hard-working."

Julie wondered how the aforesaid Mavis would feel if she could hear herself described in those words, but other considerations made her feel slightly apprehensive. It was one thing for Rhys to tell her that Mrs. Evans needed assistance, and quite another for her to take it upon herself to actually offer the vacancy for discussion in the village post office. But she had done it now, and if he was angry with her—well, it wouldn't be the first time.

"Perhaps I should mention her name to Mr. Edwards," she suggested. "Then perhaps he could get in touch with Mrs. Jones."

"I'm sure Mrs. Jones—and Mavis—would be interested," agreed the postmistress.

As she walked back to the house, Julie's thoughts were occupied with finding the easiest way of breaking the news to Rhys. It wasn't going to be easy to explain how she came to be discussing the house in the first place. He would think she had been gossiping, and in a way she supposed she had, even if her own contribution to the proceedings had been involuntary.

She had almost reached the top of the headland when she heard the sound of a vehicle behind her, and glancing round, she found a motor-cycle bearing down on her. She didn't need to wait for the rider to remove his scarf and goggles to know it was Gavin Meredith, and when he halted beside her, she turned to him reluctantly. It had been amusing to flirt with him, to exchange the kind of banter she was used to exchanging with boys back home, but her own involvement with Rhys was such that she was loath to create any further complications.

"I thought it was you," he exclaimed, pulling off his crash helmet, and running his gloved hand through his unruly hair. "I was just finishing for the day when I saw you walking up past the chapel. You should have called in to see me."

Julie's smile was perfunctory. "I wouldn't know where to find you, would I?"

"Ask anyone for Merediths, they'd know. My father has his own business, see. Painting, decorating, plumbing; you name it, he does it."

"Oh, I see." Julie hunched her shoulders as the mist drifted about them. It was much colder here than it had been down in the village, and she was looking forward to sitting by the fire and toasting her toes.

"You don't seem very pleased to see me," he remarked dryly. "I thought we might be able to fix up a date. Now that you've proved you really can leave that place!"

Julie bent her head, looking down at the plastic carrier containing the few articles she had purchased at the general stores. "It's nice of you to ask me, Gavin, but—"

"We needn't go out on the bike, you know. Not if you don't want to. My dad has a car. I could borrow that."

"It's not that, Gavin."

"What is it, then? You didn't seem opposed to the idea last week."

Julie sighed. "It's difficult. . . ."

"Oh, I see." Gavin's face assumed a knowing look. "It's difficult, is it? I get you now."

"What do you get?"

Gavin looked cynical. "His secretary, eh? Well, it's not original."

Julie gasped. "You couldn't be more wrong!"

"Making him jealous, were you? Talking to me? I'm sorry, I didn't see the *Off Limits* sign."

Julie was horrified. If Gavin started those kind of rumours in Abernarth, Rhys would be furious.

"You don't understand!" she exclaimed, and then was startled by the sound of running feet, coming from the direction of the house. They both looked in that direction, and Julie's lips parted in astonishment when William's lanky figure appeared out of the mist. He was wearing only his jeans and sweater, and the dampness had already covered his hair and clothes with moisture.

"William!" The word was torn from her, and the boy halted uncertainly at the sight of her and the leather-clad young man beside her, his expression changing from evident distress to confused incomprehension.

"Julie!" he explained, coming on disbelievingly towards them. "Oh, Julie, where have you been?"

Julie looked helplessly at Gavin and then back at William, gesturing towards the carrier. "I—I went to the village," she explained; then more forcefully: "But what are you doing? You'll catch your death of cold, coming out in this weather without a coat!"

Gavin pulled on his helmet again. "I'd better be going," he said, showing unexpected discretion, and Julie was too concerned about William at that moment to make any objection.

"Goodbye," she said absently, as William reached them, and with a distracted little exclamation, turned him back towards the house. "Well?" she demanded. "What are you doing? Where were you going?"

William shook his head wearily. "I was—looking for you,"

"For me?" Julie was startled. "But—"

"I saw you go out. I thought you were going for a walk on the beach, so I decided to follow you. But when I got down there, there was no sign of you. I came back to the house." He shrugged his thin shoulders. "I thought somehow I'd missed you. But Dulcie said you hadn't come back, and—and I got—worried."

"Oh, William!" Julie felt like hugging him, but she dared not do it. Then she sighed. "But that still doesn't explain what you were doing just now."

William shivered, and she deliberately quickened their pace, as he said: "I had to get help. I thought you might have been swept off the rocks. There's nobody but Nerys at the house, and I couldn't wait for my father to get back."

Julie took his hand in hers. "Come on," she said. "Let's run, shall we? You're frozen, and it's all my fault."

"No, it's not," he panted beside her. "I—I shouldn't have let you go out alone on a day like this. I—I've been wanting to tell you—I'm sorry, Julie."

Julie did not trust herself to answer him, and she was unutterably relieved when the lights of the house began to glimmer through the mist. Heaven knew what this outing might have done to William's constitution. If he fell ill again, she would never forgive herself.

Dulcie was waiting in the hall when they got back, and her eyes widened curiously when Julie insisted that William went straight upstairs and took a bath.

148

"You forgot your coat, Willie," she remarked, in her childish treble. "Uncle Rhys will be ever so cross."

"But you're not going to tell him, are you, Dulcie?" asked Julie quietly, shedding her own coat. "You don't do that sort of thing any more, do you?"

Dulcie pursed her lips. "Mummy says that sometimes you have to be cruel to be kind," she recited smugly, and Julie quelled the urge to tell her to mind her own business.

Instead, she retorted: "My mummy always said that what the eye didn't see, the heart didn't grieve over. Do you want to get William into trouble?"

Dulcie scuffed her toe. "You haven't taken me to c'lect any more shells," she reminded her.

"Nor shall I, if I hear any more of this. Don't try blackmailing me, Dulcie, because it won't work."

"I don't know what you mean." The little girl looked sulky.

"Yes, you do. Now, go along upstairs, William. Get your bath, and I'll order tea in the living room in fifteen minutes, hmm?"

William grinned, and it was like the breaking of a dam, allowing all the hurt and tension of the last few days to escape. "All right," he agreed eagerly, and took the stairs two at a time.

CHAPTER TEN

DURING the night, Julie heard William coughing. It was a quiet night compared to the previous week's storms, and the harsh sound echoed hollowly along the corridor between their two rooms. She came awake at once, remembering his unprotected excursion into the mist, knowing instantly that her fears on his behalf had not been unfounded. Because Dulcie had not mentioned the incident Julie had had no occasion to explain what had happened at dinner the evening before, even though she knew that sooner or later she would have to tell Rhys about Mavis Jones.

Pulling on her dressing gown, she slid out of bed and padded to the door. William was coughing again, hoarsely now as he strove for breath, and she felt a terrible sense of responsibility. It seemed that no matter how she tried to avoid it, she was involved with this family, for good or ill.

There was a light under William's door, and she halted uncertainly, suddenly conscious of the scarcity of her attire, and of what interpretation Rhys might put upon her ministrations. But when William began to cough again, she put such trivial considerations aside and opened the door.

William was not alone, however. His father was standing beside his bed, holding a glass in which some hot liquid was steaming, waiting until William recovered again. He was wearing corded jeans that moulded his lean thighs, and a navy sweater—but his feet were bare.

"Oh!" Julie's involuntary exclamation was automatic. "I—I heard William coughing. Is—is he all right?"

William nodded from the bed, forcing a faint smile. "I'm fine."

"He's not fine," said Rhys heavily, handing his son the glass again. "He's got a chill. I just wish to God I knew how. This house isn't draughtproof, I know, but I have tried to ensure that he's kept warm."

Julie hovered in the doorway, aware of William's warning eyes upon her. But it was no good. She couldn't allow Rhys to believe William had developed a cold from nowhere.

"It was my fault," she began, and ignored the boy when he tried to intervene. "I disappeared yesterday afternoon. William came looking for me."

"I see." Rhys looked down at his son again. "Is this true?" William reluctantly nodded. "Why didn't you tell me?"

"Because he thought you'd be angry," exclaimed Julie, coming into the room and half closing the door behind her, unwilling to alert anyone else to their exchange. "I'm sorry, I didn't think."

Rhys shook his head, and looked at her again, grey eyes encountering hers before moving with disturbing intentness down the length of her slender figure. Then he said quietly: "Just out of interest, where did you—disappear to?"

Julie sighed. "As a matter of fact, I walked to the village."

"To the village? But it was a foul afternoon!"

"I didn't mind," Julie defended herself indignantly. "I'm entitled to go out, aren't I?"

Rhys' eyes narrowed. "The famous *free time*," he mocked coldly. Then: "If you had wanted to go to the village, you should have told me. I'd have arranged for Haggar to drive you down."

"It wasn't necessary. I—well, I enjoyed the walk."

"Did you?"

William started to cough again, and Rhys was forced to leave his catechism of her to attend to his son. This time the bout was more severe, and with a moan of protest, William vomited the whole of his dinner, half on the bed, and half on the floor.

Rhys uttered an exclamation, and Julie waited only a moment before hurrying forward and moving him aside. "Do you know where Mrs. Evans keeps clean sheets?" she asked, reassuring William with a smile, and Rhys nodded.

"I think so."

"Well, go and get them then, while I strip off the bed."

By the time Rhys returned, his arms full of sheets and blankets, Julie had found clean pyjamas for William, and he was changing them by the fire while she dragged all the covers from his bed. The dirty sheets she had used to mop up the worst of the mess on the floor, realising they would have to be boiled before they could be used again.

It didn't take her long to remake the bed, and while she did so, Rhys disappeared again to reappear with a bucket and plenty of hot soapy water, cleanly smelling of disinfectant. He soon disposed of what was left on the floor, and Julie got a face-cloth from the bathroom, and sponged William's face and hands before putting him back into bed.

"Thank you," said Rhys, rather stiffly, when William was lying back weakly against the pillows, but Julie dismissed his gratitude.

Turning away, and speaking in an undertone, she said: "William went out without his coat. I have to tell you. But give me notice, if you like, only don't take it out on him!"

Rhys looked down at her and her heart pounded wildly at the momentary emotion that darkened his eyes. "You know I won't do that," he said huskily, and she looked confused. "Give you notice," he explained briefly. "Now—go to bed!"

Julie tossed and turned till morning. She was worried about William, concerned about her part in the proceedings, afraid that there might be something more seriously wrong with him than just a chill. But as well as these anxieties, there were others—others which put in jeopardy the whole fabric of her life here at Devil's Mount. And most disturbing of these was her relationship with its owner.

Ever since she came here, she had been aware of him, in a way totally different from any other attraction she had experienced. Her experience with men wasn't immense, it was true, but she was sufficiently familiar with the workings of her own body to know that no other man had penetrated so far into the depths of her emotions. And such a man, she thought miserably, a ruthless amoral individual, who could come from the bed of one woman and make love to another without shame or self-recrimination.

That was really the crux of the matter, she realised, as she lay there waiting for the release of morning, for no matter how he might indulge himself with her, amuse himself by arousing her immature emotions, gain a cynical satisfaction from his ability to bring the warm colour to her cheeks, it was to Nerys he owed his allegiance, and that had never been in any doubt. He had made the position painfully clear on more than one occasion, and if his honesty was hard to bear, it was because she was not like him, or his sister-in-law, unable to participate in such insincere sophistry without getting hurt. With each day that passed, she was getting further out of her depth, and that moment in William's bedroom had clarified something she had only half suspected. She was in love with Rhys Edwards, in love with a man more than twice her age, who ate little girls like her for breakfast. . . .

She was up and dressed by half past seven, and encountered Haggar in the hall when she went downstairs. The elderly manservant seemed surprised to see her, and she said quickly: "I was concerned about William. He was ill during the night."

"I know." Haggar was carrying a bucket of coals and

indicated the dining-room behind him. "If you'll come in here, miss."

The dining-room fire was already lit, and Haggar quickly transferred some of the coal in his bucket on to the blazing wood. Julie waited until he had finished rattling the shovel in the bucket, and then exclaimed: "How is he this morning? Do you know? I didn't like to disturb him."

Haggar straightened, flexing his back muscles wearily. "I understand Mr. Edwards has sent for the doctor, miss. But the boy has slept a couple of hours now, and that should do him more good than anything."

"Thank goodness!" Julie was glad she had not given in to the temptation to look into William's room. "Thank you, Haggar. Er—where is—Mr. Edwards?"

"I really don't know, miss. In his study, maybe. Sleeping, perhaps. He's been up nearly all night."

Julie nodded, and when Haggar excused himself to go about his tasks, she remained in the dining-room, standing by the fire, staring down into the billowing clouds of blue-black smoke that curled up the chimney.

William's condition got no worse, and within a couple of days he was able to get up and about again. But his illness had taught Julie a lesson she would not forget. She never went anywhere without first advising somebody where she was going.

The problem of Mavis Jones lay heavily on her mind during those days, too. Since the night in William's bedroom, Rhys had become almost unapproachable, unbending only when he was dictating to her, and even then, keeping his comments rigidly to the job in hand. Consequently, Julie did not find an opening to mention what she had done, and she lived in fear of either Mrs. Jones or her daughter coming to the house.

William was still not well enough to join her on her afternoon walks, but he was always there afterwards, waiting to have tea with her, and he manfully stifled any jealousy he might have felt when Dulcie occasionally joined them. The little girl was turning more and more to them for companionship, and there were times when Julie found it hard to relate this eager happy child to the sullen, malicious individual she had been on her arrival. She was still inclined to display that selfish, demanding side of her nature to her mother, but she knew better now than to try it on with Julie and William.

William himself seemed to have recovered from his emotional outburst, and their relationship developed almost because of what had happened. Julie felt a strong attachment to him, a deep affection, and it was this more than anything else which made her ignore the emptiness Rhys had put into her life. William needed her—and he was his father's son. . . .

One afternoon it was too damp and foggy to go out, and after she had finished working for the day, Julie went straight into the living-room where William was waiting for her. Although it was barely the middle of the afternoon, it was already gloomy indoors, and William had turned on the standard lamp to cast a triangle of warm light over the hearth.

"You're early," he said, and she nodded.

"I didn't go out. It's too damp. When this fog clears away, perhaps we'll be able to go out together."

William nodded, patting the seat beside him, and she joined him on the velvet cushions of the chesterfield. It was too early yet for tea, but it was pleasant just to contemplate the fire, knowing that she was finished for the day, with the prospect of Mrs. Evans' potato cakes and a cup of scalding tea warming the immediate future.

There were pictures in the flames, elves and goblins and all manner of weird beasts conjured up by smouldering lumps of coal. There was a dragon breathing fire, and the many-headed gorgon-lashing its tail—and yes, there was a Viking ship, long and steeply prowed, but with no lusty commander to steer it through the fiery waters. Julie sighed. She didn't think about her Viking these days. His image had been overlaid by another man's harsh visage, dark-skinned and dark-browed, with eyes the colour of the sea on a rainy day, and thick dark hair that showed blue-black, not golden, in the rays of the sun. . . .

When the living-room door crashed back upon its hinges, both William and Julie almost jumped out of their skins, William jerking his head up in astonishment from the dictionary of geological science he had been studying.

Rhys stood in the doorway, a physical manifestation of Julie's foolish imaginings, his face dark and angry as he surveyed the scene they presented. Then he moved further into the room, resting his hands on the back of the chesterfield, knuckles showing white through the skin, and she felt the first twinges of real apprehension. He was wearing black, a colour which he seemed to favour, but its sombreness only served to intimidate.

William spoke first. "Is something wrong, Da?" he asked, an unnecessary question when something so obviously was, and Rhys did not even favour it with a reply.

Instead he looked at Julie, and she wilted before the hard brilliance of his gaze. "What have you been saying?" he demanded coldly. "Exactly what have you been saying—in the village?"

Julie gasped and William looked bewildered. "Julie hasn't been to the village, Da—"

"Keep out of this, William!" Rhys was in no mood to be polite to anyone. "Well?" He did not shift his attention from Julie. "Are you going to tell me?"

Julie got to her feet. She was in her stockinged feet, but the discrepancy in their sizes seemed less overpowering when she was standing. So he had found out about the Jones girl. It was her own fault. She should have plucked up courage and told him.

"I—I'm sorry," she said now. "I know I should have consulted you first—"

"Like hell you should!" Rhys' mouth was a thin line. "For God's sake, why did you do it?"

William stood up now. "What has she done?" he exclaimed. "She doesn't know anyone in the village."

"Doesn't she?" Rhys switched his attention to his son for a moment. "What do you know about it?"

William was taken aback. "I don't think you should talk to Julie that way. What right have you—"

"Oh, William!" Rhys' fist smote the back of the chesterfield. "You wouldn't begin to understand." He paused. "This is nothing to do with you. It's between Julie and me. Now, if you want to do her—and yourself—a favour, you'll get out of here right now."

"Julie?"

William turned doubtfully to the girl at his side, and she gave him a faint, apologetic smile. "I think I know what your father's talking about, William. And—and yes, perhaps it would be better if you left us." These kind of scenes were not good for him, and already the familiar flecks of colour in his cheeks warned of his involvement.

All the same, it was like being in a battle and suddenly discovering that half your weapons were useless, and as he went out of the door, her knees started their cowardly trembling.

Rhys closed the door behind his son, and then turned to regard her with chilling penetration. "Well?" he said, folding his arms. "I'm waiting."

Julie took a deep breath. "I was in the post office, and these women were there, and they were talking about—about the house, and how it's been shut up for years—"

"Wait a minute. How did they know you were from here?"

Julie sighed. "I told them. They—they said I was a stranger. I *had* to say something."

"And?"

"Well—they said that they'd heard a rumour that the house was going to be sold—"

"What?"

"It's true. They said that—that your—your sister-in-law had never liked living here."

"That's never been in question."

"No, well—I expect they thought that she might persuade you to sell up—"

"My God! So that's why you pretended we were having an affair!"

Now it was Julie's turn to look horrified. "I—I—what did you say?"

Rhys's arms fell to his sides. "It was a stupid idea!" he intoned angrily. "You had no right to even suggest such a thing."

Julie almost choked over her words of denial. "I didn't. *I didn't!* I don't know what you're talking about."

Rhys's eyes narrowed now, and he disconcerted her still further by coming round the couch towards her. "I suppose I should be flattered really," he muttered derisively. "No one's ever done anything quite like that for me before."

"I tell you, you're mistaken!" cried Julie, staring into his dark, sardonic face. "I—I don't know what you're talking about. What has—what has this to do with—with Mavis Jones?"

Rhys's expression revealed his bewilderment now. "Mavis Jones?" he muttered blankly. "Who the hell is Mavis Jones?"

Julie put her hand to her head. A tiny throbbing had started somewhere near her temple, and the confusion she felt was disorientating her completely. "Mavis Jones," she repeated, in a small voice. "You must know who Mavis Jones is."

"I can assure you I don't." Rhys looked down at her curiously, and then put a finger under her chin to lift her face so that he could see it. "You'd better tell me."

Julie endeavoured not to succumb to the temptation to drag herself away from him. He was too close, too disturbing, she was too conscious of him to speak with real coherence.

"I—I—you wanted someone, you said so, to—Mrs. Evans can't manage."

"Take it more slowly," he advised, half impatiently. "What has Mrs. Evans to do with this?"

Julie's breasts heaved beneath the thin wool of her sweater. Forcing herself to speak slowly and lucidly, she said: "You said that Mrs. Evans couldn't manage, that she needed someone to help her with the housekeeping. So I—I mentioned it; in—in the post office."

"And this Mavis Jones applied? Why didn't you tell me?"

"No, she didn't apply," said Julie unhappily. "These women—the ones who were in the post office when I was there —they said she was looking for a job, that she might be interested. They were going to mention it to her mother."

"I see. So that was why you pretended a relationship with me? To give you the authority to employ this unknown housemaid—"

"*No!*" Julie was almost in tears now. "No, no! I—I never suggested anything like that."

"Then where has it come from?"

"I don't know . . . that is . . ." Suddenly Julie was remembering that scene with Gavin Meredith on the cliffs. His insinuations, before William had come running out of the mist and driven all other thoughts from her head. Drawing her chin away from his probing fingers, she said unsteadily: "I— I'm not sure, but—perhaps it was—Gavin—"

"Gavin—Meredith?"

She nodded, and sensed his instinctive irritation.

"You've been meeting Gavin Meredith?" His voice was hard.

"I—no." She shifted uncomfortably beneath his contempt. "That day I went to the village, I saw him, that's all."

"And he had become a nuisance to you, so you chose to disabuse him in the only way possible!"

"No." Julie shook her head, but she knew he did not believe her.

"Interesting," he murmured, and there was another note in his voice now, one which she recognised but scarcely dared to remember. "So," he said moving closer to her so that she felt suffocated by his nearness, "if I'm to be used as a deterrent, perhaps I should take advantage of the facilities offered." One hand curved round the back of her neck under the weight of her hair. "If the village is talking about us already, why shouldn't we enjoy ourselves in justifying that reputation?"

"Don't—be—silly," she exclaimed, struggling to escape from him. "You know perfectly well that I would never—"

"Do I? Do I know you so well?" he taunted her, his other hand circling her waist, spreading possessively over the lower part of her spine, as he pressed her relentlessly towards him.

It was like a scene played in slow motion, with Julie powerless to do anything to stop it. He was doing this deliberately, she told herself fiercely, desperately trying to hold on to her sanity when the intimate pressure of his thighs uncoiled that yielding weakness inside her. He was using the situation shamelessly, delighting in the power he had over her. All this was just a game to him, a sophisticated game to while away a rather dull afternoon, and while initially he had been annoyed that anyone in the village should link his name with hers, now he was realising how trivial that was, and taking advantage of what had become a rather amusing interlude.

He bent his head to hers and her hands were crushed between them, against the black silk of his shirt. Twisting her head from side to side, striving to avoid the seeking pressure of his mouth, she tried to uncurl her fingers, but only succeeded in parting the buttons of his shirt so that the fine hair which grew down to his navel was caught in her nails. She dug her nails into him then, fighting like a cat for her freedom, but her actions only seemed to incite him further and exhaustion brought the surrender of her mouth to his.

He was not gentle this time. She had fought with him, and he had overcome her struggles, had become the victor, the conqueror, with the power to do with her as he willed. His mouth was hard and demanding, his breath mingling with hers in her mouth, parting her lips until she felt dizzy with sensual feeling.

She clung to him because she did not trust her legs to support her, and felt his hands in her hair, forcing her head back so that he could bury his face in the hollow of her throat.

"You've stopped fighting, Julie," he groaned, cupping her face between his hands as she clutched at his belt. "Are you conceding defeat?" His eyes darkened passionately. "Because if you're not, I'd advise you not to trust me. Right now, I want you very badly, and although I know I'll hate myself afterwards, I don't know if I can let you go."

Julie's tongue appeared only fleetingly, and her eyes were wide and innocent as they gazed up at him. For a few seconds, they were completely absorbed in just looking at one another, searching one another's faces with an intensity that disguised completely the sudden opening of the door, and Nerys' instinctive exclamation when she saw what was going on.

But no one was allowed to ignore Nerys, and with just the right amount of sarcasm in her voice, she said: "When you've finished flattering your ego, Rhys, I'd like to have a word."

They both turned to look at the woman standing negligently in the doorway, and Julie could feel the shameful wave of embarrassment sweeping over her. She was sure that had she been in Nerys' position, she would have gone away quickly, too distresssed to intervene, and the very fact that she didn't proved the special kind of relationship she had with her brother-in-law. Perhaps she had witnessed this kind of scene before. Julie was sickened at the thought.

But before she could do anything about it, Rhys had put her aside, and was striding round the couch towards Nerys, making Julie feel as if she had been detaining him. "Well?" he said, looking down at his sister-in-law, and no one would have guessed from his attitude that only moments before he had been completely aroused, oblivious of anything but the gratification of his senses.

Nerys looked pointedly at Julie. "Would you mind?" she murmured insinuatively, and with flaming cheeks, Julie hurried out of the room.

William was hanging about on the landing when Julie went upstairs, and her heart sank at the sight of him. But fortunately he associated her hot colour with the anger his father had been exhibiting when he departed.

"What was it all about?" he asked, following her along to her room, his brow furrowing anxiously.

"Oh—nothing much." Julie was abrupt, but right now all she wanted was time to gather her scattered senses.

"Can't you tell me?"

William hovered in the doorway to her room, and turning she surveyed him resignedly. "I—well, I employed—no, I didn't employ, exactly, but I suggested that your father needed someone else to help in the house."

"When you were in the village?"

"Yes."

William's eyes brightened. "And someone wanted the job?"

"Well—maybe."

"Hey, that's marvellous! I thought no one in the village wanted to work here."

"No—well, there was this rumour, you see, that your

father was going to sell Devil's Mount. The village people resented that."

"Oh." William nodded. Then he grunted. "I bet I know who was responsible for starting that."

"Yes, well, I don't want to hear about it. The fact remains that if your father isn't going to sell the house, then I'm sure no one in the village would object to working here."

"Super!" William sounded delighted. "Then Nerys'll have even less reason for complaining about the conditions here." He sighed suddenly. "Not that that's such a good thing, of course. I don't want *her* to settle here."

"Now, William . . ."

"Well, it's true." Then he shrugged his momentary gloom away. "Oh, but that is good news about someone else working here, isn't it?" Then his brow creased again. "But I don't understand. Why was my father angry about it?"

Julie turned away, fidgeting with the cosmetic jars on the marble surface of the washstand. "He—I expect he objected to my interfering—without his permission."

"Is that what he said?"

Julie crossed her fingers. "More or less."

"Huh!" William's toe thudded into the door jamb, and Julie turned reprovingly.

"Don't do that, William." She sighed. "Now, if you don't mind, I have rather a headache. . . ."

"But what about tea?" William's cry was plaintive, but for once Julie could not respond to it.

"I'm sorry, but I don't think I could drink any tea right now," she said. "Let me lie down for a while, and I'll probably be all right by dinner time."

William was clearly torn between his desire to protest and an awareness that if he argued, Julie might not come down to dinner either.

"Oh, all right," he said at last. "I suppose I'll have to have it alone."

"Why don't you have it in the kitchen? With Mrs. Evans?" suggested Julie. "Ner—your aunt—is with your father just now."

William nodded. "I know, I saw her go in. Nosy creature! As soon as Dulcie told her I'd been sent out of the room, she came to see what was going on."

Julie acknowledged this with an inclination of her head. So Nerys had been protecting her property after all. Well, who could blame her?

Julie took some aspirin for the very real headache which had followed her confrontation with Rhys, and after resting for a while, felt reasonably well enough to take a bath. She had towelled herself, and was sitting in her dressing gown brushing her hair before the mirror when there was a knock at her door. Thinking it must be William again, come to assure himself that she was recovered, she called: "Come in!" and then felt a *frisson* of alarm slide up her spine when Nerys came into the room.

She was dressed for the evening in a gorgeous gown of dark red velvet, low-necked and long-sleeved, with bands of silver fur edging the cuffs and hem. If she had set out deliberately to make Julie feel inferior, she had succeeded, and the fleeting glimpse Julie had of her own reflection as Nerys closed the door made her defeatedly aware of her red-rimmed eyes and pale cheeks. She didn't know why Nerys had come to see her, although she guessed it was not dissociated from what the older girl had witnessed that afternoon, but she didn't see what she could say about something so obviously unimportant.

"William told me you had a headache." Nerys glanced rather haughtily round the room. "Are you feeling better?"

Julie guessed that if Nerys had acquired that information,

it was more likely through Dulcie than William. But even so, she would not have expected her to care, one way or the other.

"Thank you, it's almost gone," she answered politely.

"Oh, good." Nerys allowed a faint smile to touch her rather thin lips. "I can stand anything but a headache."

Julie acknowledged this with an inclination of her head, and waited for her to go on. Her incapacity could not be the whole reason for Nerys invading her room like this, and the earlier prick of alarm heightened into actual apprehension.

"Actually, Miss Wood, I wanted to talk to you—woman to woman, so to speak." She paused. "But this is rather difficult for me . . ."

Julie took a deep breath. "If it's about this afternoon, Lady Llantreath, then please don't say anything. What you saw—what you *thought* you saw—meant nothing, nothing at all!"

"I know that, you silly girl!" Nerys showed her teeth, but it was hardly a smile. "I should know Rhys' little foibles by now. He can't resist a pretty face, particularly one that makes it so obvious that it wouldn't object!"

Julie gulped. "What do you—"

"Oh, please, Miss Wood, spare me the dramatics! I'm a woman, too, you know, and far more experienced in the ways of the world than you will ever be, believe me. No, your—er— association with my—with Rhys doesn't really come into this. Except only indirectly."

Julie got to her feet. "Will you please come to the point, Lady Llantreath. I have to get dressed for dinner."

Nerys' lips tightened. "Very well. I understand you have been interfering in the running of Devil's Mount, that you have actually taken it upon yourself to employ some girl from the village."

"Not exactly. . . ."

"Well, whatever." Nerys' nails plucked impatiently at her long skirt. "Are you aware that I only agreed to come here on the understanding that once Rhys' book was completed, we would move back to London?"

"I don't see what this has to do with me—"

"Don't you? Don't you?" Nerys took an involuntary step forward, her eyes glittering angrily. "Then I'll explain. Having gossiped about our affairs in the village, you then boast about your success to William, filling him with the false belief that Devil's Mount is to remain his home—"

"But it is!"

"You don't know that."

"But Rhys—Mr. Edwards said—"

"What Rhys says and what he does are two different things. Once this desire for literary acclaim has left him, he'll find life at Devil's Mount a very boring affair. He's a man of the world, Miss Wood, not one of your boorish generation, who seem to find destruction so much more satisfying than making a success of their lives. He craves adventure and excitement— you must know that. What can a village on the Cambrian coast mean to him?"

"I still don't see why you're telling me all this."

"Do you not? No, well, perhaps I haven't made the whole position very clear yet. William, Miss Wood, is the cross I have to bear, and you're making it that much more difficult."

"But how?"

"You know that boy, Miss Wood. You know what he can do, how he can inveigle his own way by those imaginary attacks—"

"They're not imaginary attacks!"

"Never mind what they are. He can bring them on to order. And with you behind him . . ." She broke off abruptly. "I want you to leave Devil's Mount, Miss Wood. You're not a good influence here."

Julie's expression was ludicrous. "You can't be serious!"

"I'm afraid I am."

"But—but—I don't want to leave." Julie gazed at her

incredulously. "I—Mr. Edwards hired me. I'll leave when he asks me to, and not before."

Nerys' lips twisted. "I thought you say that."

"Then you weren't disappointed, were you?"

Julie's courage strengthened as she said the words. What could Nerys do, after all? She hadn't the authority to turn her out, and somehow she still believed what Rhys had said about not giving her notice. And there was William. . . .

Nerys sighed now, folding her arms, her fingers beating an impatient tattoo against her sleeve. "Nevertheless," she said, "I think you will leave, Miss Wood. If you don't, I shall have no choice but to tell William that Dulcie is not his cousin, but his *sister*."

CHAPTER ELEVEN

THERE was silence in the room for a full minute after Nerys finished speaking, and when Julie finally did manage to say: "I don't believe you!" her voice was curiously hoarse.

Nerys shook her head indifferently, and a cold blankness descended over Julie's mind. "I don't think it matters whether you believe it or not, Miss Wood. But William will."

"His father will deny it!" Julie burst out chokingly.

"As he denied his own son's birth, no doubt."

"You—you're evil!"

"No, just honest, Miss Wood. Don't tell me you haven't suspected it."

But she hadn't. Never for one moment had such a thought crossed her mind. And yet now that it did . . .

She shook her head violently, as though to shake away the visions Nerys' words had evoked. She could imagine what this kind of revelation would do to William. His relationship with his father was still such a tenuous thing. And Nerys was right—he would believe her, even if she was lying.

"Why are you doing this?" she cried now, and Nerys stretched out one arm and examined her nails with calculated deliberation.

"I have no intention of mouldering away at Devil's Mount while Rhys satisfies some sentimental desire to relive the days of his youth. Oh, yes, Miss Wood," this, as Julie's face mirrored her contempt, "I know what Rhys is trying to do. Did he tell you why? No? Well, I suppose he wouldn't at that. He can be irritatingly reserved when it comes to talking about himself. But I don't have his hang-ups—"

"Please, I don't want to hear—" began Julie, her hands

clenching and unclenching impotently, but Nerys ignored it.

"It has to do with me, of course. But you probably guessed that. Both the brothers were in love with me, you know, but Richard was the elder—he would inherit the title. And I was ambitious. It was foolish—I realise that now. Rhys always had more gumption than Richard. Besides, he was the one I really wanted. Only I thought I could have both."

"Will you get out of here?" Julie did not know how much more of this she could stand, but Nerys hardly seemed to hear her.

"When I married Richard, there was the most terrible row between the brothers, and the upshot of it all was that their father, old Lord Llantreath, ordered Rhys out of the house. And he went, unfortunately, to Africa—and India—and Vietnam; wherever there was a war going on. That's quite something, isn't it? That a man should try to get himself killed because the woman he loved had chosen somebody else?"

Her lips curled smugly.

"I think it's—sick!" burst out Julie chokingly. "I think you're sick!"

Nerys looked at her pityingly. "Why? Because I've exploded all your girlish dreams? Surely you realised I didn't come here because of the climate!"

"I really don't care why you came here!" retorted Julie tremulously.

"Don't you? Don't you really? Forgive me if I find that hard to believe. You're attracted to Rhys, Miss Wood. It stands out a mile. And I must admit I'm becoming a little bored by it." She paused. "But let me finish my story—"

"I'd really rather you didn't."

"—when their father died, seven years ago, Rhys came home for the funeral. Richard was—prostrate with grief,

169

helped a little by the bottle of Scotch he managed to consume most days, and I—well, I needed consolation—"

"Don't go on!"

"Why not? Fortunately, Richard was too drunk most of the time to know what I was doing, or what he was doing, for that matter. Rhys was a—tower of strength."

Julie bent her head. "All right, all right. You've said enough. I believe you."

"So you should. After all, Richard and I had been married for eight years without producing the expected son and heir. Whereas Rhys already had one illegitimate child, fathered on a girl from Cardiff when he first discovered I was going to marry Richard."

Julie held up her head. "Just tell me one thing, Lady Llantreath, what will you do if William still throws a scene when he knows I'm leaving?"

Nerys' raised dark eyebrows. "I shall leave that to you to arrange. But if you want my advice," she paused, "I should just make my arrangements and leave. You can write William a note. There's not much anyone can do about a *fait accompli.*"

"But how can I do that? It's twenty-five miles to the railway station."

Nerys shrugged. "I'll telephone for a taxi for you. You can leave the bill to me."

Julie sank down wearily on to the bed. "You've got it all worked out, haven't you?"

Nerys nodded. "Yes, I think perhaps I have."

Julie did not go down for dinner that evening. Not even a desire to allay William's suspicions could force her to make an effort at swallowing food which she was sure would choke her, and besides, she needed time to think.

Nerys had not left her much choice in the matter. Her threats had been only too well voiced, and there was no one to whom Julie could turn for advice or guidance. She did consider going to Rhys and making a clean breast of the matter to him, but would he be able to silence Nerys, or would she find some devious way of letting William find out the truth? It was a risk Julie could not bear to take. Just recently, there had been a definite improvement in the relationship between William and his father, but the revelations she had heard this evening could shatter all that in the twinkling of an eye. William was so sensitive, so quick to take offence, so vulnerable in the matter of his parentage.

She wondered how much time Nerys would give her. Not long, she guessed. She had been a thorn in the woman's side long enough, not only over Rhys but over Dulcie as well. She had made it obvious that she disliked Dulcie spending so much time with Julie and William, but Rhys' presence had made it impossible for her to put her objections into actual physical terms.

For Rhys himself, Julie still felt a terrible sense of longing. In spite of everything, she still loved him, and after what she had heard today she did not think anything would ever alter that. It was a daunting thought that for the rest of her life she was doomed to live with the memory of a man who had treated her, and life, with scant respect.

She was making a desultory attempt to sort out her belongings when William came to her door. She knew it was him at once because she heard him call: "Julie!" through the door, and with a sinking heart, she said: "Come in."

She was still wearing her dressing gown, having put on her underwear but nothing else, and he looked in surprise at the clothes strewn on the bed.

"What are you doing?" he asked.

Julie shrugged. "Just—sorting things out."

"I thought you had a headache. You didn't come down for dinner."

"I wasn't hungry. You know how it is."

"But you didn't even have a cup of tea this afternoon!"

"It will do me good. I'm getting too fat." Julie tried to speak jokingly, but failed dismally.

William looked at her anxiously. Then he said perceptively: "What is it, Julie? What's wrong?"

She coloured. "Nothing. You know how it is when you have a headache."

"You look as though you've been crying. Have you?"

"No!" Julie sighed. "I think I've got a cold coming on, that's all."

William looked unconvinced. "Why did Nerys come to see you?"

"Nerys?" Julie was aware of the guilty expression she was wearing, and hoped he would not put the wrong interpretation on it. "How do you know that Nerys came to see me?"

"I was on my way here before dinner, when I saw her knocking at your door." He coloured now. "I listened outside for a while, but I couldn't hear what was going on."

Julie breathed a sigh of relief. "You know what they say about eavesdroppers."

"I know. But—well, you have to admit it was unusual. She doesn't normally come visiting you."

"No." Julie sought around wildly in her mind for some excuse to make. "I—someone had told her I had a headache. She came to see how I was feeling."

William looked sceptical. "And I'm Count Dracula! I don't believe that."

"Well, I'm sorry."

"*Julie!*" He looked at her reproachfully. "I'm not that green, you know." He chuckled. "But I bet she was."

"What do you mean?"

"This afternoon. I bet she was mad when she found you and Da in the living-room."

"What do you know about that?"

"You know what I know. I was there! I told you—I saw her go into the room."

"You mean—you were—there? In the hall?"

"When she opened the door, yes." William hung his head. "Yes. I saw you with my father. I wasn't going to mention it, you know."

"Oh, William!"

"Well, I don't really mind," he went on slowly. "At least, not as much as I did before. I mean, I'd rather it was you than Nerys, if you see what I mean?"

"Oh, William, you couldn't be more wrong!"

"Why? Da likes you, I know he does. He told me."

Julie wanted to question him about that, but she was too used to quelling these kind of feelings. Instead she said: "Well, I'm glad you feel that way, William, but so far as your father and Nerys are concerned—I don't count."

William pursed his lips. "Did Nerys tell you that? I bet she did. I bet that's why she came here. To tell you to keep away from him!"

"I think you've been reading too many stories, William!" exclaimed Julie severely, her heart pounding, even so.

"No, I haven't. I know what she's like. She's mean and spiteful and—"

"Stop it, William!" Julie put her hands over her ears, her nerves strung to screaming pitch by his acute perception. "She could become your stepmother one day, and it won't help—"

"*She won't!*" William interrupted her fiercely, and although he spoke violently, there was no sign of his usual breathlessness. "Da wouldn't have her years ago, before she married Uncle Richard, so I'm sure he wouldn't marry her now."

"You don't know what you're saying, William," she exclaimed, but it was a feeble remonstrance and he knew it.

"Yes, I do. You think I don't know about my mother, don't you? Well, I do. I know she left me in a children's home Dulcie told me that ages ago. And when I asked Da just recently, he said it was time I was told the truth." He sighed "She was a lot older than he was, you see—my mother. H met her in Cardiff, and—I suppose they must have loved on another—for a time. Then Uncle Richard married Nerys and Da went abroad, and it wasn't until he came back and went to find her that he found out about me."

Julie found her throat was dry. William had such a touching sincerity, and it was so much easier to believe him than t believe what Nerys had said. But who was telling the truth?

"Well—he brought me out of the home," the boy wa saying steadily, "and he found someone to care for me while he was away. I—I didn't see a lot of him in those days, but knew he was there, and that he must have wanted me or h would have left me in the home, wouldn't he?"

"Yes, William."

"But when I was older, when I wanted to go abroad wit him, he made me go to school. It was all right for a time, but was never any good at games, and sometimes I'd get so upse that I couldn't breathe. That was when it was discovere that I had this nervous asthma, and I'm afraid I used to use it shamelessly."

"To get yourself expelled?"

"Yes." William shook his head. "I thought that if I wa expelled enough times, Da would relent and take me wit him, wherever he went."

"But—wasn't he fighting in—in wars, and things?"

"He was a mercenary for a time," agreed William, nodding "but after being injured in Central Africa—"

"Injured?" Julie couldn't deny the automatic response.

"Yes." William frowned. "An African fractured his spin with the butt of his rifle."

"Oh, but I—" Julie broke off, her hand pressed to her throat. "I—something like that happens in—in the book."

William didn't look surprised. "I expect it does," he remarked casually. "It's all true, you know. Or as much of it as he dare publish. That's my father's story you're typing, Julie. Didn't you guess?"

Julie's legs gave out on her, and she sat down with a bump. Of course! She ought to have guessed. There was so much in the book that only first-hand knowledge of a similar situation could have made possible. And the man Barnabas, the man she found so endearingly honest and humane, matched exactly the image she would like to have had of Rhys. . . .

"I've read it, you know," William added proudly. "Da said not to mention it to you, not until it was finished, but I think he wouldn't mind, in the circumstances."

"Oh, *William!*" There seemed nothing else to say.

"So whatever Nerys has said to you, ignore it," he concluded. "She's getting fed up with being here, and now that Da is going to employ some more people, I think she's realising that he won't be shifting back to London at the drop of a hat." He grinned. "Perhaps she will be, though."

Julie didn't know what to think. Was it possible that this new William, this increasingly confident William, might find it possible to weather the storm of his father's infidelity? Might he find it in his heart to forgive him for something that had happened seven years ago? Or would Nerys' revelations destroy everything? And if so could she, Julie, take it upon herself to be the arbiter of his fate?

Late that night, after William was safely in bed, and the house was settling into silence, Julie still paced the floor of her bedroom. Nerys had not come to see her again as she had half suspected she might, but she knew that in the morning the problem would have to be resolved, one way or the other. But

175

the idea of walking out, of leaving both William and his father to discover her apparent treachery, sickened her.

And yet she could see that it was a way out. If she attempted to confront William with the news that she was leaving, and he attempted to stay her, she didn't know if she would have the strength to withstand him.

She went to the window and looked out. It was a clear frosty night, much different from the afternoon it had been, the cold air sharply defining the curve of the headland. A pale moon illuminated the breakers rolling into the shoreline, and with a pang, she realised that she might never walk on that shoreline again.

With a feeling of inevitability she shed her robe and pulled on her jeans over her underwear, adding a thick sweater for warmth. Then her tweed coat completed the ensemble, the scarf wound round her neck, imprisoning her hair in its folds.

The house was silent as she stole down the stairs, and she was reminded of that other night she had crept down here when the wind had been howling through every nook and cranny. Tonight there was no wind, just the sighing of the sea below the headland.

Haggar had bolted the door, and it wasn't easy to draw the bolt. But she succeeded at last, and turning the key, let herself out the door. She had never been out in the dark before, except in the lighted streets of a town, and there was something rather terrifying in the awareness of her own vulnerability.

She ran lightly down the two flights of steps, and circled the house, keeping to the gravelled footway. Rhododendron bushes looked eerie in the moonlight, a hiding place for intruders, and William's earlier remark about Count Dracula came back to haunt her.

But she thrust such fanciful thoughts aside, and reaching the cliff edge, began the descent to the beach. It was jarringly cold and she was glad of her scarf to keep her ears from freezing. But her hair blew wildly about her face, and she had to keep wiping strands of it out of her mouth.

Down on the rocks it was a little less cold, the frost tempered by the salty tang of the sea. She stood for a while just staring towards the horizon, taking great breaths of the keen air, hoping for some inspiration to clear the confusion in her head. But at least one thing had been explained to her. She knew now why sometimes Rhys moved so stiffly, and the image evoked by William's blunt words of a rifle butt in the back brought goosebumps out all over her flesh.

When she heard the sound of pebbles tumbling down the cliff, she did not immediately associate them with anyone's approach. But an awareness that she was no longer alone and unobserved, made her glance round, and her heart caught in her throat at the sight of a dark figure quickly jumping down the face of the cliff.

She remained where she was for a moment, frozen with shock, but then the lateness of the hour, and the fact that the house had been in darkness when she left, forced her to the possibility that he could be the intruder she had thought about earlier.

With a gulp, she looked about her. There was no escape. The beach stretched ahead of her, bare and uninhabited, but ending in the blank wall of rock that formed the headland. Moonlight illuminated her position with the clarity of a spotlight, but the shadowy figure was shrouded in darkness.

"Who is it?" she called jerkily, her voice faint and faltering. "Who's there?"

"Well, it's not Count Dracula!" answered a laconic voice, and her breath escaped from her on a deep shuddering sigh.

"*Rhys!*" she breathed, unaware of the feeling in her voice at that moment, and he vaulted down the final curve to the path to land on the rocks beside her.

He must have jarred his back because he uttered a low

oath, but it was only a momentary spasm before he strode towards her, his expression rather daunting in that pale light.

"What do you think you are doing?" he demanded, stopping right in front of her, and she thrust her hands into her pockets so that he should not see how they were shaking.

"I—I could ask you the same thing," she countered, and he shook his head.

"I came after you," he said, and she tried not to read more into those words than there really was.

"How—how did you know . . ."

". . . that you were down here?" She nodded. "I saw you from my study window."

"Oh!" Julie swallowed hard. Then another thought struck her. "Why—why did you say that—about Count Dracula?"

His lips twisted. "Isn't that what William said to you? When you told him Nerys had come to your room to enquire about your health?"

Julie gulped. "Will—William told you about that?"

"Of course."

"I see."

"Why shouldn't he?"

"N—No reason."

He regarded her intently, seemingly unaffected by the cold even though he was only wearing a dark battle jacket over his shirt and pants.

"Tell me something," he said quietly, "did you believe what he told you?"

"What who told me?" she cried, playing for time.

"William." His eyes narrowed. "Don't play games, Julie. I want to know. Did you believe him—or Nerys?"

"What do you know about Nerys?"

Rhys sighed. "Enough. Enough to know that after what I told her this afternoon, she did not come to see you for any philanthropic reason."

178

Julie stared at him. "Wh—what did you tell her?"

"I asked you a question."

Julie pursed her lips. "I—I believe that William believes what he told me."

"What's that supposed to mean?"

Julie bent her head. "It's not supposed to *mean* anything. I'm just reassuring you that William has no doubts—"

"Damn you, I don't need your reassurance!" He was breathing quickly. "I know my son, Julie. Maybe not a lot better than you do, but some. I told him the truth, for what it's worth. I have never lied to him."

Julie acknowledged this silently. Then she said quietly, "You don't have to explain yourself to me."

He swore then, and she took a step back from him. "I know I don't *have* to explain myself to you, but I want to!" he muttered. "Have the decency to listen."

Julie shifted her weight from one foot to the other. "It's nothing to do with me," she protested, knowing that every word he said was deepening the eventual pain of parting.

"I disagree." His eyes glittered. "You ought to know the truth.

"Oh, what does it matter?" she exclaimed defeatedly.

"I want you to know why I did what I did."

Julie's shoulders sagged. "I know what you did. You left Devil's Mount when you found that Nerys was going to marry your brother, and—and consoled yourself by making some girl in Cardiff pregnant!"

Her voice had risen as she spoke, and when she was finished the silence seemed that much more tense. How had she dared to say those words? she asked herself in dismay. She who had always endeavoured to remain impartial in all things.

Rhys expelled his breath on a heavy sigh. "So that's what she told you," he said flatly. "And you believed her."

Julie moved her shoulders helplessly. "Isn't it true?"

179

"Well, the facts are all there. The way they were presented might bear some examination, though." He paused. "I presume Nerys told you that I didn't want her to marry Richard?"

Julie nodded.

"Well, I didn't." Julie's heart slumped. "But not because I was jealous." He shook his head. "It's so easy to misconstrue the facts. It's like one of those problems that has more than one solution. You have to decide which solution is the logical one." He raked a hand through his hair. "I can just as easily say that Nerys married Richard to spite me. That fits the facts, too."

Julie shivered. "And William's mother?"

Rhys nodded. "Oh, yes, William's mother. I'll get to her. But first, just in case you have any doubts about Nerys' story, I should tell you that I was engaged to her—once." Julie's eyes widened, and he gave a rueful grimace. "That surprises you? It shouldn't. Nerys always was a beautiful woman. And I was young and inexperienced—immature, if you like. But it didn't take me long to discover what she was really like, selfish—self-seeking—mercenary, and—cold."

"Cold?"

"Yes. Cold." Rhys' lips twisted. "Emotionless—in any normal sexual way. I think the word they use today is frigid."

Julie gasped. "But—but—"

"I eventually broke off the engagement. You can imagine the furore that caused. Arrangements for the wedding were already under way, and my father was furious. He said I was making a fool of him—of the whole family. He demanded that I change my mind or—get out. I got out."

"Oh, Rhys!"

She was hardly aware of using his name, but he went on: "You can guess what happened. Richard was not as strong as I was. My father could intimidate him. He married Nerys in my stead, and lived to regret it."

Julie remembered what Nerys had said about Richard's drinking. Was it possible that there was some other reason for that? As Rhys had said, facts could be twisted to mean anything.

Now Rhys moved stiffly, as if the cold was getting into his bones, and Julie said hastily: "We should go back," but his hand on her wrist kept her there before him.

"Not yet," he insisted. "There's still the question of William's mother."

"You don't have to go on—"

"Oh, but I do. Because she was no innocent either. But she had more heart than Nerys could even imagine." He paused. "I could lie and make up some tale about her being just a girl I met and spent some time with. But I won't insult you by altering the events to suit the occasion. She was a nightclub hostess, Julie. Need I say more? But she had a heart of gold, and for some reason she seemed to care about me. Sufficiently so not to take the necessary precautions."

Julie quivered in his grasp. "I see."

"Do you?" His voice was harsh. "I doubt it. Anyway, she had some religious beliefs—a hangover from her chapel upbringing, I suppose. When she found out that she was pregnant, she had the child, even though I was long gone. You probably know the rest. She left him on the steps of a children's home. I found out when I came home from Vietnam, and I—rescued him." He hesitated. "Perhaps you think I should have married her. But I don't think she wanted that. She was quite a lot older than I was, and set in her ways. We were just two strangers who for a brief period of time gave each other companionship. When you've been in the places I've been in, when you've seen the sights I've seen, you realise that that means a hell of a lot."

Julie could not bear to look at him then in case he should see the emotion in her eyes. So William had not been born out of hatred, as Nerys had denounced, and if not out of love, then at least from an unselfish need.

Rhys released her wrist suddenly, and she started. "What's the matter?" he demanded savagely, and she realised he had misunderstood her silence. "Has my story shaken that romantic imagination of yours? Oh, yes, I've watched your face when I've been dictating. I've seen the disenchantment there. Well, life isn't a tidy thing. People don't ride around on white chargers rescuing maidens in distress any longer. Such knights as there are, are knights errant, searching for other causes far more deserving! I'm a flawed gallant, Julie, and it's time you grew up!"

Julie stared up at him then through tear-swept eyes. "I am grown up," she told him tremulously. "I grew up the first time you kissed me."

"Did you?" His expression remained sceptical. "Another ball on my chain, would you say?"

"What do you mean?"

"Oh, Julie, don't you understand anything? I want you! I've wanted you for a long time. But I'm too old for you, and besides, I don't want a blinkered child to hold in my arms!"

Julie gulped. What was he saying? Did he know what he was saying? Had he tired of Nerys now and thought to put her, Julie, in the other woman's place? Oh, God, she thought, am I strong enough to live the rest of my life knowing I have eschewed heaven? And there was still Dulcie.

She took a couple of steps back from him, unconsciously seeking the cliff path behind her, and his eyes darkened.

"What is it now?" he demanded. "What else has Nerys said about me?"

"Wh-why should she have said anything?"

He took a step towards her, his eyes narrowing. "Because I think I know you, Julie. I know you're not indifferent to me. So what else is there between us?"

But she could not tell him. With the words hovering on her tongue, she could not speak them. *What if they were true?* a voice hammered inside her head. Would they not then cast doubts on everything else he had said?

She had to get away from him, she thought unsteadily. She had to get away before emotion swamped common sense, before she found herself giving in to a man who could never give himself wholly to anybody.

With a stifled sob she turned away, and ignoring his command to wait, she began climbing the path to the clifftop. She tried to run and stumbled as she went, and with an exclamation heard him coming behind her.

But halfway up she heard him utter an oath and stumble the rest of the way down again, and she turned from her position just below the rocky shelf to see what had happened. He had stumbled off the rocks on to the beach, and from where she was standing he appeared to be kneeling on the sand.

"Rhys?" she called doubtfully, aware of an immense sense of responsibility flooding her being. "Rhys? Are you all right?"

He did not answer, and her stomach plunged sickeningly. "Rhys?" she called again. "Rhys, at least tell me that you're all right."

But only her own voice echoed round the cove and with a clenching of her fists, she started down again. Her hair blinded her at times, and she thrust it back impatiently, quickening her step as she neared the bottom and saw that he was now lying on his back on the sand.

"*Rhys!*" she cried, rushing over the rocks towards him, and going down on her knees beside him. "Rhys," his eyes were closed, "Rhys, speak to me!"

"I love you," he said, to her complete astonishment, and his arms came up around her, pulling her down on top of him.

His hand at the nape of her neck guided her mouth to his,

and in her shocked state she could not suppress the desire to give in to him. His mouth was so warm and demanding, moving on hers, his body hardening beneath her until she uttered a little protest and broke away from him. But not far—he would not let her go and with a lithe movement which belied his injury, he drew her down on to the sand beside him and turned to straddle her body with his own.

"I'm not going to let you get away," he groaned. "Not until I've said everything I came to say."

"But—but your back—"

"I only jarred it. But as you seemed so concerned, I thought I'd let you come and comfort me."

"Why, you—"

She wanted to be angry with him, but with the heat of his body protecting hers from the cold, his hands inside the tweed coat, hard and possessive, she found it incredibly difficult to resist him.

Tears of helplessness trickled from the corners of her eyes, mingling in the moistness of their mouths, and he licked them away curiously, saying: "Come on, Julie. I need you so much."

"But—but Nerys—"

"What about her?" A harshness invaded his tone. Then a certain comprehension appeared in his eyes. "Of course—you think—I *let* you think we were lovers."

"L-let me think."

"Of course." His voice hardened. "Julie, if it was anything else, I would tell you. You've got to know me, Julie. You've got to understand that sometimes I may say things you won't like, but I'll never lie to you."

"But that night—in the kitchen—"

He half smiled. "My angel of mercy! Oh, Julie, if you had had any idea of what you did to me that night. . . . I had to say something, I had to drive you away. But then William did it for me."

"William—"

"—will love his new mother."

"His—mother?"

"Well, stepmother, then." He frowned. "You will marry me, won't you? I mean—oh God!" He stared at her in mock irritation. "You didn't think—but yes, I can see that you did. Julie, how many more times must I say it? Nerys was lying . . . I never touched her after she married my brother!" He sighed. "And marriage still means something to me. I don't offer it lightly."

"Oh, Rhys!"

She couldn't hold out against him any longer, and as his mouth possessed itself of hers, and his body surged against her, she knew that she believed him at last, and nothing Nerys could do could alter that. . . .

When they walked back to the house, their arms around one another, there was still one more question Julie had to ask.

"What will—Nerys do?"

"When we're married, you mean?" Julie nodded and Rhys drew her closer against him. "You may not believe this—"

"I will," she insisted, and he smiled.

"—but the day after you arrived, I contacted an estate agent in Llantreath who had connections in London, to arrange for an apartment for her. She doesn't like it here, and now I've finally convinced her that she's wasting her time with me, she'll go."

"Is that what you told her this afternoon?"

"Yes." He paused. "I wanted her out of the house before I told you I loved you, but in the event, her intervention precipitated things. I knew she'd try to make trouble for us, and I wanted to avoid that."

Julie bit her lip. "She—she told me something else. I—I

have to tell you. I can't have it between us."

"What?" Rhys' eyes were dark.

Julie drew slightly away from him. "She—she told me—Dulcie was your child—that when you came home for your father's funeral . . ."

"*What?*" His disbelief was violent as his fingers dug painfully into her shoulder. "God, what must you have thought of me?"

Julie moved closer to him again. "I—she wanted me to leave. She said I should just—go. Without first telling you."

"Yes, that would have suited her." Rhys clenched his fists. "But don't imagine that would have been the end of it. I would have found you, wherever you were."

Julie looked up at him. "W-would you?"

"Yes." He frowned suddenly. "But come with me. I want to show you something."

They went into the house quietly, and let themselves into the library where first Julie had known that devastating awareness of this man who was going to be her husband. Taking some keys from his pocket, he unlocked the desk drawers which she had always been told to ignore. He extracted a file, and a handful of papers.

"Look," he said, and she found herself staring at two certificates; one was his father's death certificate, the other belonged to Dulcie, giving the date and place of her birth.

"You don't need to do this," she protested, guessing what was to come, but he ignored her.

"Read this," he instructed, thrusting another paper into her hand, and she read the medical reports of his injury during fighting in a Central African struggle for independence. The intimate details of his injuries made her feel sick to her stomach, and she looked up at him helplessly, but he insisted she went on. And then she knew why. He had been in hospital when his father had died, and could not possibly have attended

186

the funeral. Dulcie's birth some eight months later confirmed that she could not possibly be his daughter.

"Oh, Rhys!" Julie exclaimed bitterly, "you didn't need to do this."

"I had to," he said simply, and the look on his face turned her lower limbs to water. "Sometimes it's necessary to prove something to oneself."

Julie understood. She also understood that she need have no fears for William now. Nerys could not harm any of them ever again.

Six months later Julie, Rhys and William were seated round the fire in the living room, sharing afternoon tea as Julie and William had used to do in those early days.

"Oh, it's good to have you back again," William exclaimed, grinning at his father and his stepmother happily. "But I'm glad you had a good time. Was Jamaica very hot?"

"Very hot," agreed Julie, looking down with satisfaction at the golden tan she had acquired. "Next time we go, you'll come, too."

Rhys lay back in his chair looking with satisfaction at his lovely young wife and at his son's animated face. "So the school isn't so bad?" he commented, and William shook his head.

Since their marriage, three months ago, he had been attending a private day school in Llantreath, and now that he had a home to come back to every night, he was working well again.

"Oh, by the way," William got up to fetch a letter which had been lying on the mantelshelf, and handed it to Julie. "This came for you a few days ago. I think it's from Dulcie."

"Dulcie?" Just for a moment, Julie felt a twinge of remembered anxiety, and Rhys stretched out a hand to close over her wrist.

"Do you want me to read it?" he asked quietly, but she shook her head.

"No. It's all right. I just wonder why she's writing to me."

Since Rhys had announced his intention to marry Julie and Nerys had walked out of the house, their only contact had been through the medium of solicitors.

But Dulcie's letter was endearingly friendly: *Dear Aunt Julie*, it read, *I hope you and Uncle Rhys had a nice holiday. We live in London now, and I go to school with another little girl who lives in the same flats we do. I like living here because there's proper heating, so Mummy says, and there are two bedrooms and I have one all to myself. When I was at Uncle Rhys' house I had to sleep with Mummy because she said it was so cold. Lots of love, Dulcie.*

Julie handed the letter to Rhys after she had read it and saw the way his lips twitched. Then he looked at her and she knew he was thinking the same as she was thinking. Then he handed the letter to William.

William read it with a degree of his usual cynicism where Dulcie was concerned. "Oh, well," he said, "at least she's happy anyway."

"Aren't we all?" said Julie, lifting her shoulders and allowing them to fall with the sinuous grace of a cat that has just had the cream.

What readers say about Harlequin Presents

"I never enjoyed love stories until I started reading Harlequin books."

"Who ever would have thought that so much pleasure could be found in such a small package."

"Thank you for having the type of books that people can enjoy reading over and over again."

"Security is having six new Harlequins on the shelf waiting to be read."

*Names available on request

Harlequin Presents...

The books that let you escape into the wonderful world of romance! Trips to exotic places...interesting plots...meeting memorable people... the excitement of love....These are integral parts of Harlequin Presents— the heartwarming novels read by women everywhere.

Many early issues are now available. Choose from this great selection!